A TAX IN
BLOOD

A Tax in
Blood

Benjamin M. Schutz

This is a work of fiction. All the characters and events portrayed in this book are fictional, and any resemblance to real people or incidents is purely coincidental.

A TAX IN BLOOD

Copyright © 1987 by Benjamin M. Schutz

First printing: January 1987

A TOR Book

Published by Tom Doherty Associates, Inc.
49 West 24 Street
New York, N. Y. 10010.

Cover art by Jill Bauman

ISBN: 0-312-94421-7

Printed in the United States of America

0 9 8 7 6 5 4 3 2 1

For my parents, with love

Acknowledgments

I would like to thank the following individuals for the gracious donation of their expertise: Ronald L. Thompson, D.V.M.; Carlos Mejias of the Olde Towne School for Dogs; Maurice Vargas, Department of Public Affairs, OAS; F. Barton Evans III, Ph.D.; Neil Ruther, attorney at law; Mark Schutz, M.D.; Officer Adam Schutz, MPDC.

Doubt is not a pleasant mental state
but certainty is a ridiculous one.
　　　　　　　　　　　—VOLTAIRE

To die for an idea
is to pay a high price for conjecture.
　　　　　　　　—ANATOLE FRANCE

A TAX IN
BLOOD

Chapter 1

THE BLACK WALL is something to see. It appears before you, unexpected but no accident, like Stonehenge does on the green English fields. To get to the wall you pass a statue of three fighting men. Like Cerberus, they guard their dead comrades. Though there are other ways to the wall, if you don't pass by their fierce gaze you are sneaking in.

Arnie, Samantha and I stopped in front of them and silently requested permission to pass. To my eyes their gaze was an accusatory one of equal parts anger, hurt and disbelief. "You sent us there. This is what happened to us. Did you get what you wanted? Was it worth it?" The questions tolled off in my mind like cathedral bells signalling noon. I had no answers on my tongue, just a thickening in my throat.

Samantha laced her fingers in mine, and we went down to the wall. Arnie had moved slowly away from us. He was casually dressed except for the blue and white ribbon around his neck and the medal that hung from it. Mirrored sunglasses kept the world at bay.

As we approached the wall I began to read the names of the dead men. We descended below ground, and the names began to pile up. Soon I could read only one name on each line of a panel. Then only one name on one line of a panel. It was too much. There were too many names and they multiplied faster than I could count them. I looked up. Ahead, it was a long way to the bottom. Each panel was larger than the one we'd passed. I turned to go back the way we'd come in and was surprised at how far in we were. There was no way out except past the dead: the ones behind us or the ones ahead.

Further on Arnie had stopped. He stood at attention and snapped off a salute. He'd found a friend. Nearby a small boy stood looking up at him. The boy backed away and without taking his eyes off Arnie reached up for his mother's hand.

As we marched up the incline, I fought off the impulse to look away. Each name fought to make a personal claim, but the numbers undid that. It was simply too much. I looked down at the base of the wall. Here and there small flags were stuck in the dirt, along with flowers and pictures. I squatted down to look at a photo. *Here's your daughter Tammy Sue. She's real proud of you* was scrawled underneath a school portrait. I shook my head. Though Samantha had walked along with me the entire way, I felt utterly alone.

Another veteran in a wheelchair passed us. He looked about my age. I felt vaguely embarrassed that I was not maimed. His arms were folded uselessly in his lap and an older, white-haired woman was pushing him along. Though his head lolled unsteadily as he rolled past, above his red beard his gaze was piercing and clear.

The woman with the small boy who had been standing next to Arnie reached up to touch the wall. Slowly, fingers touching stone, she traced a name like a blind person does the face of a loved one. Tears streamed down her face, and for a moment she staggered and pressed her head against the cool stone.

I went up to Arnie and put a hand on his shoulder. He did not stiffen nor did he acknowledge it.

With his arm around his mother's leg the boy continued to stare up at Arnie.

"That's my uncle's name up there. He was a hero in the war. Were you a hero?" the boy asked.

"No, son. I was just lucky."

The boy's mother straightened up, wiped at her tears and reached down to stroke her son's head. She sniffed back a tear and said, "It's my brother he's talking about. Jimmy's a little heavy to pick up that high. I wonder if you could lift him up so he can see his uncle's name and touch it. I named him after my brother. Keep the family name alive and all that." Her voice had a slight Southern drawl.

Arnie reached down and picked the little boy up under the arms. He held him aloft like an offering to a silent god.

"What's his uncle's name, ma'am?" he asked.

"James Tucker Calhoun."

"Just like me. That's my name, too," the boy crowed.

Arnie scanned the wall for a moment and found the name. "Here it is, Jimmy. Your uncle's name. Reach out and touch it. Pay your respects." The little boy reached out and traced it just as his mother had done. When he was finished he snapped off a small salute, like he'd seen Arnie do.

Arnie gave him back to his mother. She thanked him and let her eyes wander over him, searching for a mark perhaps or anything that would explain why this man had come back and her brother hadn't. Arnie turned away after a clipped wave to little Jimmy and we three trudged up from the depths of the wall.

We walked across the gardens, past the kiosk and pool towards our cars. In the distance a group carrying placards was marching in a circle. When we got closer, I read the messages: ONCE WAS TOO MUCH, NO MORE VIETNAMS, LEAVE CENTRAL AMERICA NOW, CIA ADVISORS TEACH DEATH. A fifteen-year-old case of paranoia made me visually sweep the area looking for FBI crew-cuts taking pictures, compiling dossiers. Original sin runs deep, and even studying history doesn't seem to help us.

We crossed Constitution Avenue to our cars. Arnie stopped at his, turned his back to us and put his key in the door lock. Samantha reached out and put her hand on his shoulder. When he turned back she said, "Arnie, I can't believe you can come here and just walk away like this. I mean, I've been trying not to cry the whole time and I wasn't even there. I know you have feelings. Don't keep them all to yourself. We're your friends. Let us . . ."

Arnie just stared at her. "You don't know what you're

talking about. What you see is what you get." He turned away, opened the old Nova's door, slid in and closed us out. When the motor turned over he rolled down the window and said, "Thanks for coming down here with me. That's what I needed, nothing else. If and when I need more I know who to ask and how to ask. See you at the dojo tomorrow, Leo." With that he pulled away.

I slid an arm around Samantha's shoulder. "You all right?" I asked.

She looked up and smiled weakly. "Yeah, a little stung is all. Why is he like that? He's so damned cold. He's like a machine."

"He's a samurai."

"I know. I know, that's what you say about him all the time, but what the hell is that supposed to mean?"

"When I say Arnie's a samurai, that's not quite true. He can't be. This isn't feudal Japan and he wasn't raised from the cradle to be a warrior. Underneath that shell there's still twenty years of corn-fed American dreamer. What he's added on is the Japanese idea of *giri* or debts of obligation. All relationships in Japan are based on them. They must be discharged to maintain your honor. For the samurai, or warrior, that means a commitment to death before dishonor."

"But why hold on to that code now? The war is over. He acts like he's still at war with everyone. Doesn't he know how to make peace?"

"Not until he makes peace with himself. I think that the samurai code was a piece of field surgery he did on himself over there. Maybe he's afraid of what will happen if he shucks that armor now. I don't know."

Samantha shivered as a gust of wind blew up. "Can we continue this discussion in the car?"

"Sure."

I let Samantha in and walked around the car. She reached across and unlocked my door from the inside. I slid in and turned the engine on.

"What did you mean when you said 'field surgery'?" she asked.

"Field surgery just keeps a guy alive, or in one piece until he can be medevacked to a real hospital where they try to repair the damage. Adopting the samurai code makes a lot of sense when you think about the war."

"How so?"

"The samurai pursues something the Japanese call *makoto* or purity of spirit. This purity of spirit means acting totally on impulses from the core of your being, unpolluted by calculating reason. Right or wrong is not as important as a pure heart. To risk death on a quest that cannot succeed is the perfect task for a samurai as a test of his *makoto*. If that isn't a thumbnail sketch of the Vietnam War I don't know what is. I think adopting that code gave Arnie a way to salvage some meaning out of a situation that for lots of people had deteriorated into absurdity. He wove that code pretty deeply into the fabric of his being; he had to. I'm not sure he can put it aside now."

She sat for a while, thinking. "Okay, I understand all that, but you know sometimes I'm not sure if he's looking for a way to live or a way to die."

"I'm not sure he sees a difference. In his dojo there's a sign that says 'Practice dying every day. You get only one chance to do it right.'"

"God, what a way to live." She shook her head.

We crossed the Memorial Bridge into Virginia and took I-395 South through Arlington to the Duke Street exit and Samantha's apartment. As we pulled up in front of her building I tried one last time to talk her into being irresponsible and having dinner with me.

"Leo, I can't and you know it," she said. "This manuscript is due in New York by Tuesday and I have a ton of work left to do on it. I shouldn't have come out today but it was important. Now I need to hole up with this and get it done. Please let me finish my work. I'll be a lot more fun to be around when it's off my mind."

I nodded in resignation. "Okay. Call me when it's done."
The giveaway that I had no chance was when she said
please. It's her way of asking me not to make her say no.
She'd do it if she had to but she'd rather not. We kissed
good-bye and I drove home.

Chapter 2

As soon as I got in I went over to the television and turned it on. The Dallas game would be starting soon. My stock with Samantha had gone up appreciably when she found out that I had a share in season tickets to the Redskins games. Unfortunately I'd lost the toss to my brother. He and his latest honey were at the game. Twenty-five years ago when my father first got them, you couldn't give away Redskins tickets. Now the waiting list for them is measured in eons. Holding a pair of them can boost your social standing tremendously. They exempt you from the required years of breeding and wads of money. At least from September to January they do.

I went into the kitchen as they announced the one-hundred-and-forty-something consecutive sellout of the stadium. Fifty-five thousand screaming fanatics created such an adrenaline contact high that playing at home was worth damn near a touchdown to the Redskins. I put some leftover pizza in the microwave and opened an Anchor Steam beer. As I watched the camera pan around the stadium at the fifty-five thousand cheering faces, I was jolted by the image of a skull in every seat. That's how many names were on that wall: a sellout at RFK. What a waste. We don't kill people anymore, we "waste" them. Just ask any punk on the street.

When the pizza was hot I took it and my beer to the living room and tried to get lost in the game. The Redskins were eating up the yards and the clock. The ball was on the three yard line and everyone in Washington knew it was going to Rogers behind the Hogs. Knowing it and stopping it are worlds apart. Rogers took the ball and headed towards Grimm and Jacoby. Between them appeared a hole a yard wide. I leaned forward ready to cheer. Suddenly the picture disappeared. SPECIAL NEWS REPORT flashed on the screen. I was staring at the face of a local anchorman.

"We interrupt this broadcast of the Redskins-Cowboys football game to bring you this emergency report from the Vietnam Veterans Memorial." He touched the receiver in his ear. "Dick, are you ready? Okay, go with it."

The next picture was of a reporter standing on the grassy knoll opposite the wall. He was repeatedly running his hands through his hair and there was a stain on his shirt the camera couldn't avoid.

"Minutes ago, a bomb, apparently hidden in a picnic basket, exploded here at the Vietnam Veterans Memorial. The police have cordoned off the area and are holding everyone in the immediate area for questioning." The howl of an ambulance rose above his voice. Cries and wails could be heard over that. He went on. "We're going to try to get closer to the wall if we can. What you hear are the survivors." He began to walk down the path we had taken towards the wall. The minicam eye followed him. A police officer held up a hand and halted them. After a brief conversation, the reporter turned back. "We're not being allowed any closer. We're going to try to pan the scene from here."

I stared at the set, fascinated and horrified. Rubbernecking at a crash site. You missed me. You missed me. There but for the grace of God, go I. To feel the chill and still live. The camera zoomed in. The wall was pitted and scarred. Many of the names had been obliterated by the shrapnel. Whole panels were cracked in jagged lines. As the camera's merciless eye crossed the wall closer to the ground, you could see stains on the wall, pools in the dirt and then the slowly spinning wheel of an upended wheelchair. Paramedics with stretchers were crisscrossing the screen. Each body they carried was sheeted head to foot.

The camera moved back to the reporter's face. "The

death toll at present is nineteen. Five others have been sent to Georgetown's Shock Trauma Center. That's all we know at this time. We will have updates whenever new developments emerge. We return you now to our regularly scheduled program."

I finally took a deep breath, got up out of my squat and went back to the phone. I called Arnie. The phone rang four times before he picked it up.

"Yo."

"Arnie, did you hear about the wall?"

"No. What?"

"A bomb went off just after we left. It tore the place up. Nineteen dead, five more critical."

"Who did it?"

"Don't know yet."

"What about the kid and his mother?"

"No names have been released. They might not have been there either."

"Okay. Thanks for calling."

I tried Samantha. She wasn't answering her phone. Damn.

I finished eating and sat staring at the set. I had achieved the rare anti-Zen state of being both empty-headed and muddled. The countdown of the final seconds and the roar in the background brought me around. The Redskins had won and the hated Cowboys would have to skulk back to Dallas and lick their wounds. I couldn't have cared less.

Promptly at seven the news came on. Sitting next to the anchorman was a D.C. police officer introduced as Lieutenant Calvin Simmons. After the introduction and an open-ended question, Simmons began to flesh out the earlier report.

"The device was a large explosive charge wrapped in a casing of metal balls. It seems to be homemade, but the design is similar to the 'Bouncing Betty' mines that were used by U.S. forces in Vietnam. The size of the charge and its configuration allowed for a uniform saturation across the entire face of the wall. The choice of explosive, its placement and the timing of the detonation indicate that the intention was clearly to maim and kill those visiting the memorial, not to damage the structure itself. We believe the bomb was detonated by remote control, and are requesting that all photographs taken by people at the memorial today be brought to us for enhancement. Hopefully, someone will show up in the background either with the picnic basket or observing the wall from the hillside facing it."

The anchorman cut in. "Has anyone claimed credit for the bombing?"

"No, not yet. Because the site of the attack is federal property we are coordinating our efforts with the FBI. The last two attacks on federal property in the city were both bombings of the Capitol. In 1971, the Weathermen claimed responsibility for a bombing in protest of the strategic bombing of Laos. In 1983 a group calling itself the Armed Resistance Unit set off a bomb to protest our involvement in Lebanon and Grenada. However, in neither of those attacks was anyone killed. This kind of attack, launched without warning, signals a new level of terrorist activity in the city."

"Thank you, Lieutenant Simmons. We are switching now to our remote cameras at the Shock Trauma Unit. Come in, Dick."

The reporter I'd seen earlier came back on. He didn't look so hot.

"Uh, yes. We don't have much on the five people still in critical condition. Three are still in surgery. However, next of kin of the other victims have been reached and we can release those names now."

A roster of names began to roll across the screen. Two thirds of the way down the names of James Tucker Calhoun, age eight, and Melissa Anne Calhoun, twenty-seven, of Knoxville, Tennessee, rolled by. Rest in peace.

The news switched back to the studio and became a background drone and irritation. I turned it off and tried Samantha's number. Again no answer. In the kitchen I poured a couple of inches of John Powers Irish whiskey and took my current reading, Allen Wheelis's *The Illusionless Man*, to my easy chair.

Try as I might I couldn't forget James Tucker Calhoun's sudden end. Unbidden, his image would flash onto my inner eye. First positive, then negative, then gone. I ached around the edge of his absence, like the pain from a phantom limb. Not a great pain. We had only passed a few minutes together, but it was enough to lift him from the nameless, faceless crowd into my memory. I stared at the ceiling and yearned for Arnie's armor. Instead, I settled for John Powers's undercoat and glaze.

Chapter 3

I WOKE UP in the chair and then tried to get the kinks out in a stinging shower. That done I went into the kitchen, flipped on the coffee and brought in the newspaper. Page one led off with a story that AIDS was now being declared a "punishment from God" for homosexuality by certain religious leaders who obviously had the Almighty's confidence. Further down was the announcement that General Hortencio Villarosa was coming later this week to sign a treaty with the U.S. We were giving him weapons and advisors to subdue the Communist guerillas in his country in exchange for stepped-up activity against the cocaine kingdoms in the highlands. Between these two stories there was a brief follow-up report. Two of the initial survivors had died during the night, and no one had stepped forward to claim responsibility for the carnage. Security was being increased at all borders and major airports. A group of Libyans had been sighted somewhere. Libyans, the boogeymen of the '80s. I had a bagel and cream cheese with my coffee. After eating and flipping through the entire paper I called my answering service.

The only call of apparent significance was from Nathan "The Mad Bomber" Grossbart of Grossbart, Shaftweiler and Nicoletti. Nate was a graduate of the University of Napalm School of Law. Unfortunately, he practiced domestic law. Dozens of family therapists stayed in practice trying to put back together what he had managed to put asunder. If all gall is divided into three parts, Nate got two of them. He argued each case as if the kingdom of heaven was at stake;

and make no mistake, he was on the side of the angels. That status was immediately conferred upon his receipt of the retainer. Rumor had it that he required sedation before he could settle a case. What was significant was that he had called me. I'd never worked for him before — wouldn't — and he knew it. I tried to recall ever being married and drew a blank. He wasn't representing an ex of mine, thank god. The call intrigued me. Maybe he'd really screwed up somewhere and needed help personally. A long shot, that. "Straight Nate" was his other nickname. The man without vices and much the worse for it. I dialed his office.

"Law offices."

"Nate Grossbart, please."

"Who shall I say is calling?"

"Leo Haggerty."

"Thank you. Hold please." I got Muzakked.

"Leo, Leo. How's it going? Are you free to talk today? I've got something interesting for you. Can you come up to the office, say noon?"

"Excuse my reluctance, Nate, but considering our past disagreements, what on earth do you have that I could help you with?"

"It's not a divorce. I know, I know, we don't see eye to eye on that. But this is different. It's murder." He said it like a small boy saying "fuck" for the first time. He was right though; I was interested.

"Your side, the doer or the done to?"

"Neither. A helpless victim herself."

"First off, Nate, no contingency deals. Cash and carry or it's bye-bye." Nate and his money were parted as often and as easily as the Red Sea.

"Okay, okay. Have it your way. What do you say? Noon, today?"

"Pleasure talking to you, counselor. I'll be there at noon."

Chapter 4

AT THE DOJO I dressed in the changing room. As I walked across the padded practice floor to the dirt sparring area, it occurred to me that I hadn't seen Arnie anywhere. He was always here before me and usually meditating when I arrived. In my left hand I carried my weapon of choice: *kusari gama*, the sickle and chain. A two-foot long ironwood baton with a curved sickle at one end and a weighted fifteen-foot length of chain at the other. My practice baton had a wooden sickle blade. Hefting it, I began a series of drills: feints, lunges, whirling attacks, slashes, combinations going forward and backward. Still no Arnie. I was pretty well warmed up when I saw him enter from the far side. He walked across the pounded dirt floor in his usual splay-footed manner.

"How ya doin'. I've been here fifteen minutes or so."

Arnie bowed and drew one of his swords. Like Musashi, the "sword saint," he taught a two-sword school. He held it before him and began to circle me. This was odd.

Casually, I lifted up the baton and began to twirl the chain. "Aiyee!" Arnie screamed, raised his blade overhead and ran at me. His blade ripped through the air and I leaped to the side, dragging my ball and chain. Arnie hopped over it, spun around and began to come at me again. This time he was windmilling his blade before him like a berserk sushi chef. I was tottering backwards and barely got my baton up in front of me to block his blow, the force of which drove me sharply backwards. Even though his blade was wooden it could be lethal in his hands.

"What's the matter with you, man?" I yelled.

Nothing, just the same intense, expressionless mask for a face. Maybe he's finally snapped. A flashback. Maybe he thinks I'm Charlie. Holy shit. "Arnie, it's me — Leo, your friend. American," I said, tapping stupidly at my chest. He bellowed again and came at me with a quick series of scissor-legged lunges. Instinctively, I began to whirl the chain. He backed off. I let out more chain and it whooped in an arc of death. This is my space. I control it; enter at your own peril. I adjusted my grip on the baton. This was crazy. This was nuts. I tried to reason with him again. "Arnie, talk to me. What's happening?" I began to get paranoid. Maybe he'd been hired to kill me. By whom? "What'd I do?" Nothing. I racked my brain, trying to figure out why he was doing this. "What is it, man? We can work it out, whatever it is."

"Aiyee!" Arnie ran at me again. Tentatively I swung the chain at him, trying to ensnare his legs so that I could try to disarm him. He easily evaded my toss. I hastily coiled the chain again. We circled each other. He held his blade high and began to inch towards me for another lunge. I had an idea. Come on a little closer, just a bit. My eyes flicked from his face to his feet. Slowly, I let out chain between my fingers. One more chance to end this without blood. He took that last step. I snapped the chain up and at him with a flick of my wrist. There was enough chain. It looped around his blade. I yanked it towards me, but no! I hadn't caught the hand guard. He slipped the blade free and ripped a backhand blow into my right arm. It went numb. I backpedaled as quickly as I could. Jesus, Jesus, Jesus. I'm facing a guy who thinks he's a seventeenth century killing machine. I can't believe this. Arnie's low growl drew me back from that thought. Shit. I shifted the baton to my right hand, gripped it low on the handle and held it chest high. Once again I began to swing the chain. Fuck the reasons, you want to kill me, you crazy bastard, come and get me. I ain't rolling over for you, old buddy. I began to whirl the chain in ever faster figure eights between us. I flexed my right arm and tried to get some feeling back in it. If I could keep him at bay until I could use the arm and the sickle, I might be okay.

Arnie took a step backwards and drew his second sword. I kept sweeping the air and flexing my arm. Suddenly, Arnie stuck his blade into the arc of the chain. The chain wrapped itself around the blade. I yanked Arnie towards me and raised the sickle. He drove the tip of the entangled blade deep into the ground. I tried to free the chain. With a leaping pirouette he came down with both hands on his other sword and that raised high over his head. "Aiyee!" he roared and ran at me. I was stuck in place. I couldn't move. I was nailed to this spot by his other blade. His sword flashed downward. I raised the baton overhead to block it. His blow shattered it. I was dead. . . .

And then Arnie tapped my head ever so lightly and leaped behind me. He slowly sheathed his blade, bowed to me and dropped down to sit cross-legged. I was utterly defeated and naked in my fear. Dead but not buried, I was unable to rouse even puzzlement, much less gratitude for his last act.

I looked down at my hands and dropped the broken pieces of the baton to the dirt floor.

I looked over at him and said through clenched teeth, "What the fuck was that?"

"Today's lesson."

"Today's lesson?" I bellowed. "Are you out of your fucking mind? You could have killed me!"

"Congratulations. You have mastered today's lesson, albeit slowly."

"Fuck you, sport." I stalked away. "I thought we were friends. How could you fuck with me that way?"

"Precisely because we are friends. For whom else would I have taken such a risk? I knew that this was only a lesson, you didn't. To save your life you would have killed me at the end. I know it. I could see it in your eyes."

"Goddamn right I would have. You still haven't answered my question. Why?"

"Because you insist on asking that question."

"Fuck you, asshole."

"All right, tell me this first. What did you learn here?" Arnie got up to his feet.

"I learned never to trust anyone again."

"Stop it. Don't be petulant. Think. Don't dishonor what has happened."

"What did I learn? Okay. I learned that I spend too much time thinking about why things are happening and not enough about what's happening. At the end I didn't give a shit about why you were doing it, just that you were, and I was ready to kill you, but . . ."

"But . . ." he prodded.

"But it was too late. By the time I was ready to fight back I was dead. Too little too late."

"That's right and that's the point. Think about yesterday's bombing. There won't be any distinction between peace and war anymore. Anywhere, anytime, without warning you could be history. The most ordinary routine activities are the most dangerous ones. The ones you approach full of assumptions about who's a friend or a foe, the ones where you don't notice that brown bag over there or that the car parked at the corner has a ticket on it. Those who don't respond immediately and totally to a threat, who don't keep their eyes and ears open, will die with all sorts of interesting questions on their lips. And I, friend, don't want you to be one of them. You're too interested in motives. That's a luxury you can't afford anymore."

"Maybe." I sat there nursing a slow burn. Good lessons sure, but I didn't like the way I was learning them.

Arnie went on. "What did you learn about strategy?"

"Shit, I don't know. You surprised me, catching the chain like that. When you stuck it in the ground I was tethered to it. The weapon controlled me."

"Exactly. You were ensnared by your own snare. Musashi always counseled attacking the enemy's strength. There is a weakness in all strength and a strength in all weakness if you can turn it to your own ends . . ."

Visions of yin-yangs danced in my head but I couldn't hear Arnie anymore. I was too pissed off to be enlightened.

"All this samurai bullshit sounds good, Arnie, but I can't

shake the feeling that you're talking to yourself. It's you who doesn't know the difference between friends and foes. Yesterday you took a bite out of Samantha, today it's me. Look around, buddy. You don't have any other friends. I don't know what's going on, but I do know that I'm pissed as hell and I need to put some distance between us until I cool off." With that I turned my back to him and walked away. When I left to go to my car he was still standing there.

Chapter 5

TRAFFIC BRAIDED ITS WAY on and off the ramp as I entered I-270 for the drive down to Nate's office in Georgetown. Forty-five minutes later I was inching through gridlock looking for a place to park and swearing that I was going to start using the subway.

The law offices of Grossbart, Shaftweiler and Nicoletti, P.C. were in one of the new waterfront restoration complexes that overlook the Potomac, a river so polluted that it's been declared a national historic toxic waste site.

I parked my car in the lot a block up from Nate's office and joined the hordes packing the sidewalks. Lunchtime in Georgetown, quite a spectacle. Corporate St. Georges in their hand-tailored pinstripe armor and lances by Gucci, side by side with punksters in Day-Glo mohawks and push-pin earrings. The sidewalk cafés were full of matrons from Bethesda and McLean, dressing up, lunching out, putting a new gilt edge on their boredom. Insulated behind layers of money and prestige, their world ended at their finger-nails. And nary a black face. This may be "Chocolate City," but the cake still has a white buttercream icing. I wandered past a shop specializing in hammocks, recliners and remote control devices. It was called the Joggernaught: the world at his fingertips for the man who hardly moves.

The law offices were on the fourth floor, overlooking the Whitehurst Freeway just upstream from the Kennedy Center. The receptionist showed me right in to Nate's office. He sat with his back to me, admiring the view from his office window.

Nate swirled around. "Leo, Leo. Good to see you. Have a seat. Mrs. Donnelly, uh Vasquez, will be here any minute."

"She the client?"

"Yes, a lovely girl." Nate had come around from behind the desk, pumped my hand and guided me to a chair. He sat on the corner of his desk. Nate took the high ground instinctively.

"I'll wait until she gets here to fill you in. You won't have to ask any questions twice. Time is money, right?"

When it's yours, Nate, it's like blood. "While we're waiting, Nate, let me ask you one question. Why not use Carmine?"

"Carmine's a putz. He couldn't find his ass with both hands and a map. If he wasn't Nick's nephew I wouldn't give him dog shit to bury."

"Tough with Nicoletti being your partner. He still trying to blackmail clients?"

"Where'd you hear that? That's slander, Haggerty. I won't have it."

"Cut the shit, Nate. I don't know how you've kept his ass out of the slammer, but Carmine's a legend by now."

"And what, off the record of course, is that 'legend'?" Nate crossed his arms in a huff.

"Let's see, the book on Carmine goes like this: Good on photo work but tries too hard for skin shots. Rumor has it that he keeps copies of the good ones. Can kick the hinges off any standard door, and he's a real terror if you're naked. A dedicated professional. He'll even hire a girl for the guy, especially if the client is running out of money. Waves his gun around way too much, almost as much as he flaps his gums. The ayatollah doesn't have as many enemies as Carmine claims to. Fancies himself quite the cocksman. I hear he has a sexual rebate offer for female clients. I can go on."

"That's enough, believe me. I do my best to control his 'zeal' for this kind of work. When he's on a case for me, he knows I won't tolerate any of his shit."

The door clicked as it opened and Mrs. Donnelly/Vasquez

walked in. She was dressed all in black from her high heels and patterned stockings to her taut skirt and the broad-shouldered jacket over her café au lait skin. She wore a wide-brimmed hat and no smile. We shook hands, and she introduced herself as Marta Vasquez. When she sat down she took off her hat and put it in her lap. Her hair was as black as her dress. It was pinned up in a chignon. Bitterness coated her face like lacquer. With large intense eyes like onyx chips, a proud scimitar nose and full, blood-red lips, she was dark, fierce and hard. A "lovely girl," indeed!

"Very good, very good. Now that we're all here, let me explain the situation to you, Leo." Nate had gone back around to his side of the desk. I slid a glance over at Mrs. Vasquez who hadn't warmed up a degree. I was getting frostbite on that side of my face. Oh well. I looked back to watch Nate as he told his story.

"Mrs. Donnelly, uh Vasquez, asked me to represent her in divorce proceedings against her husband, Malcolm Donnelly. This was a couple of months ago. A typical divorce battle. He was being quite unreasonable, but that's neither here nor there. On Friday, Ms. Vasquez, uh that's her maiden name and we're petitioning for its return to her, was meeting with me to discuss the assets that she might lay claim to, when all of a sudden, her husband burst into this office making all kinds of wild accusations." Nate stopped theatrically. I was on the edge of my seat with anticipation. I wished I had some popcorn.

"Such as?"

"Such as"—Nate beamed, thankful for such an invitation—"that she was an unfit mother, that he could prove it and would, that he'd never let her have custody of their children, and that he'd just begun to fight."

Wonderful, John Paul Jones gets a divorce. "And then?"

"The next day the police call Ms. Vasquez and tell her the man's killed himself. Can you believe that?" Nate puckered his mouth and slapped his palms down on his desk. I took that for total disbelief.

"That solves your problems, Nate. No divorce, no property settlement, no custody battle. Where's the beef?"

Ms. Vasquez answered me. I steeled myself for the diarrhea of a mad housewife. "The beef, as you put it, Mr. Haggerty, is that my husband systematically squandered our assets over the years in his foolish efforts to advance his career and his other 'hobbies' and left me with the kids, the debts and, of course, his final gift." She clenched her teeth and rapped out her rage with clicking nails on Nate's rosewood desk. "A case of, how you say, the clap."

Nate smoothly stepped in. "The only unencumbered asset was a two-hundred-thousand-dollar life insurance policy. However —"

I waved Nate off. "Ms. Vasquez, I'm sorry I was so flip. Please accept my apology." She nodded slightly.

Nate went on. "However, it's less than two years old, so the standard suicide clause is in effect."

"How did he die?" I asked.

"He had some medication and alcohol in him. Died of respiratory failure."

"Why not put it down as accidental?"

"Because there was a letter found at the scene."

"Typed or written?"

"Typed, but signed apparently. I haven't seen it yet."

"That's pretty flimsy stuff to hang a suicide finding on."

"I know, but the M.E.'s office has been under a lot of pressure lately. Seems that too many prominent people have suffered questionable 'accidental' deaths recently. Some of them are going to have to go down as suicides, and this one looks good enough to them. The insurance company loves it. All we've got is that twenty-four hours prior to his death Malcolm Donnelly was in this office threatening us with all sorts of legal battles. Not at all like a man at the end of his rope, ready to end it all. He was damn sure that he had Marta here dead to rights on this unfit mother charge. No way in hell was he suicidal. That's what I want you to prove."

"When you called yesterday you mentioned murder. Do you have anything to support that notion or is this the old bait and switch, Nate?"

"Would you have come over so quickly if I'd said anything

else? Time is of the essence on this case. I wanted to get you here to hear me out. What do you say?"

"All right, I'll take the case." I struggled with the impulse to shaft Nate on the fee. His contingency deal with Ms. Vasquez would probably gross him close to sixty thousand dollars. I held to my standard rate. "Three-fifty a day plus expenses."

"Reasonable expenses," he countered.

"No way, Nate. Jesus'll be back before 'the reasonable man' shows up. You'll pay my expenses, period."

Nate said okay. He was in obvious pain.

"Who was the investigating officer?"

"A Sergeant Sproul. Wilfort Sproul. He's assigned to the second district."

"All right. He'll be my first stop. I'll prepare a contract for services. Have one of your couriers pick it up at my house first thing tomorrow. I'll come by for it and a three-day retainer about noon."

"I'm in court all day tomorrow."

"Okay. I'll be here at five-thirty. Have it ready or I walk."

"No problem."

I got up to leave and turned to the widow. "One question. How did your husband know that you'd be here?"

"I told him. Under the terms of the temporary custody decree, he was to pick the children up at the house at three-thirty. It was his turn to have them for the weekend. I told him that I'd be late picking them up from school, that he could get them after four o'clock. He asked me why I was going to be late so I told him. I guess I shouldn't have but I was tired of having to answer to him."

"Okay. I'll be in touch as soon as I find out anything." I could tell she was thrilled. I left her one of my cards and let myself out.

On the way down to my car I thought how easily and predictably Nate had gotten me to his office. Just holler murder and here comes Haggerty. It made me sound like a vulture. I wasn't sure I could argue with that.

Chapter 6

I RANSOMED MY CAR and took M Street out of Georgetown. Once around the circle at George Washington University Hospital to Pennsylvania Avenue, then down past ground zero and across the mall towards the river and the police station.

In the lobby I asked them to ring Sgt. Sproul. The officer at the switchboard handed me the phone. "Vice. Schwartz here," a voice rasped.

"Uh, I was trying to reach Sgt. Sproul in homicide."

"Hold on."

"Sproul here."

"Sergeant, my name's Haggerty. I'm a private investigator retained by the family of Mr. Malcolm Donnelly to investigate the cause and manner of his death. Would it be possible to see a copy of your report?"

"Yeah, come on ahead. I'm doing it right now."

"Fine." I handed the phone back to the switchboard man who got confirmation from Sproul. "Take the staircase at the end of the hall. Homicide's on the third floor. Sproul's off at a corner desk," he said.

"Thanks," I said and went off to find Sgt. Sproul.

Wilfort Sproul was as black, hard and shiny as anthracite. His bony face gleamed, courtesy of a malfunctioning heating unit that had turned the third floor into a sauna. In shirt and shoulder holster he typed away at the report. After the barest acknowledgment of my presence, he said, "Have a seat. Be with you as soon as I finish this thing."

I sat down, took out my note pad and flipped it open.

Sproul leaned back, cracked some vertebrae, pulled a pack of Luckies out of his shirt pocket and said, "Let me see your license." I took it out of my wallet and handed it over to him. "Who hired you?"

"Nate Grossbart. He's representing the family."

"What's his number?"

I gave him the number. Sproul called Grossbart and got confirmation of our relationship. He put down the phone, lit up a Lucky, yanked the report out of the carriage and handed it to me.

It was straight to the point. Malcolm Donnelly checked into the Presidential Arms on Fourteenth Street at three P.M. on Friday. He was alone and took a room for the night. He made no long distance calls and did not eat dinner at the hotel. The next morning, at approximately eleven A.M., the maid entered his room and found him sitting in the chair next to the night stand. He was quite dead. The investigating officer found no signs of violence, or of forced entry. No one had come to the desk asking for Mr. Donnelly. His car had not left the garage. The parking sticker stamped 2:52 was still on the windshield. Mr. Donnelly had not gone down and requested a cab to take him anywhere. He apparently hadn't left his room at all. It had rained all Friday afternoon and evening. The clothes he wore were unwrinkled and there were no water marks on his shoes. The desk clerk identified them as the clothes Donnelly had been wearing when he checked in. He had no raincoat or umbrella. His wallet was in his coat pocket with thirty dollars cash and all his credit cards. Nothing seemed to have been stolen. No, Mr. Malcolm Donnelly quietly, civilly, peacefully, checked into a hotel, went up to his room, closed the door, sat down and died. The end.

I looked at the copy of Donnelly's bill and the picture of his car with the sticker still on it. I noted the maid's, doorman's and desk clerk's names.

"Were you the officer on the scene?"

"Yeah."

"So, all the stuff here about property, clothes and so on, you personally saw and okayed?"

"Yeah." Sproul's eyes narrowed and he blew smoke out of his nostrils, slowly.

"Who was the M.E. on this?"

"Carrington."

"Is the report ready?"

"Not yet. I can tell you what the preliminary said."

"Which was?"

"He had some pills and booze in him. Tranquilizers or antidepressants. He apparently checked in with a bottle of gin in his bag, had a few belts, popped some pills, sat down and just stopped breathing."

"He drinking alone?"

"Yeah, one glass used, and the others accounted for. No sign of any company at all."

"Where'd he get the pills from?"

"Don't know. Didn't have the bottle on him. M.E. said there were just traces though. Some kind of fluke reaction."

"Doesn't that sound like an accident?"

"Yeah, but I still got that letter to account for."

"Tell me about the letter."

"Same old, same old. You've seen one you've seen 'em all. Life sucks and I can't take it anymore."

"Can I see it?"

"It's down with the M.E. When his report comes up the letter will be attached. You can see them both then."

"Suppose I told you that this guy's wife says he was itching for a fight just the day before, promising a bloodbath in court and making all kinds of accusations?"

Sproul smirked. "I'd say it's just her and her shyster lawyer. They've got an insurance policy riding on this finding. Gimme a break. We've got a cause of death and two choices: accident or suicide. I've got a note at the scene. Typed, sure, but it's signed. I can't see it any other way and neither can the M.E. Go back to your client, tell her she married a shit and he's shafting her from the grave. That's tough but that's the way it is. I've got work to do. Queer over on Ransome Street wound up a fruit salad in his trash compactor. Lover's quarrel, no doubt." Sproul dismissed me with a backward wave of his hand.

I got up and left. Trotting down the station house steps, I remembered the old joke about the Southern Sheriff's verdict when a cement-clad, bullet-riddled black man was dredged up from his river: "The worst case of suicide I ever saw." I didn't think Sproul would like my point.

Chapter 7

IN THE CAR I made some notes. I wanted to see the M.E.'s report and the letter. I'd ask Ms. Vasquez about her husband's clothes and wallet. Most of all I wanted to reconstruct Malcolm Donnelly's last day. Somewhere between Nate Grossbart's office and the hotel room I just might find out why he died. Last but not least, I thought I'd ask the receptionist at Grossbart, Shaftweiler and Nicoletti to tell me about Malcolm Donnelly's visit. I used my car phone to call the hotel. No one that I wanted to talk to was on duty. They'd all be there tomorrow, I was assured. I got Marta Vasquez's number from Nate's secretary and called her. No answer.

It was a little after three. Pretty soon the city's arteries would start to clog up and all the drivers would get hypertensive. Traffic jams make me crazy. I decided to beat the herd out and head for home.

I pulled into my driveway before four, scooped up my mail and let myself in. Dumping the mail on the kitchen table, I called my answering service. No messages. I flipped through the mail. This month's *Video Newsletter*, *Washingtonian* and *Rolling Stone* went into one pile. The junk mail I stacked up and tossed out. I opened the bills, arranged them by due date and put them on my desk. There was one check. I gave that a big kiss.

I poured myself an inch of John Powers, sat at my desk, typed up a contract for Nate Grossbart and called his office. "This is Leo Haggerty. Please have your courier service pick up my contract for Nate Grossbart at my office at nine A.M."

"Of course, Mr. Haggerty. Mr. Grossbart left instructions for that. Could you confirm the address?" She read it off to me.

"That's right."

"Fine. Our courier will be there at nine."

"Very good." We hung up.

I transcribed my notes and made up a file headed VASQUEZ/DONNELLY. Back in the kitchen I scooped up my magazines to read and put a Talking Heads tape on. When I was done reading, I turned the television on for any further word about the bombing at the wall.

The six o'clock news was signing on when the special report logo appeared. Oh Christ, here were go again. The reporter on screen was from a Los Angeles station. "A bomb has gone off atop the interchange of the Hollywood, Harbor-Pasadena and San Bernardino freeways. The bomb was apparently what is called an F.A.E. bomb, or fuel-air-explosive. The explosion blew out the roadbed causing it to collapse on the lower levels. The ignited fuel set fire to the cars on the road. Those that were unable to stop in time fell through the holes, crushing cars below. A number of people were trapped in their cars as the fireball spread. Others abandoned their cars and fled on foot. Traffic in this area is backed up for miles in all directions. Even where I am you can feel the heat. It's incredible. The police are asking people to stay put so that emergency vehicles can reach the disaster site. From where I am you can see the central fire and the twisted concrete and metal of the road-beds. They look like the charred carcass of some giant animal. Every once in a while a smaller fireball appears when a car's gas tank explodes. You can see people climbing over wrecked or abandoned cars, trying to stay ahead of the flames. Now you can hear sirens in the distance. It's just too hot to go in after people. Unless they can get out by themselves, there's just no way to help them."

I turned the television off. A new stop has been opened on Trans-Terror Airways. See America and have a blast!

In the silence I felt the first tendrils of the terror planted among us.

I got up and wandered through the house, round and round, like a piece of unclaimed luggage. My agitation was as much from missing Samantha as it was from the terrorist attacks. I knew from yesterday that reading wouldn't distract me so I locked up and drove over to Tysons Corner to see *Aliens*. As promised, it got my attention. I watched the movie twice, once to be frightened and once to savor the damnedest movie about motherhood I'd ever seen.

I sacked out around eleven and slept well until I dreamt that I was riding a horse through a narrow canyon. As the canyon became ever narrower all the riders had to move into a single file. Slowly we crept through the canyon, unable to speed up or turn back. In the distance I heard a whooshing sound followed by long screams. Finally, I looked up the sheer sides of the canyon walls and saw a giant standing astride the ravine. As the riders passed between his legs his giant blade came down and cut the riders in half. I looked around for a way out but there was none. No way to turn back, and no way out of the canyon. I looked up and saw the giant sword descend on me. I was. . . . awake. Bolt upright and panic-stricken at three A.M., I tried to forget that the giant had Arnie's face.

Chapter 8

MY RESIDENT JAZZ WOODPECKER woke me with his syncopated rat-ta-tat-tat. I was considering taking a shot at him, when the phone rang. Reluctantly I picked it up. "Hello."

"Mr. Haggerty, this is your answering service. A Ms. Vasquez has been calling. She'd like you to call her immediately."

I took down her number. "Thank you."

Wonderful, wonderful. I levered myself up to a sit, stood and walked into the bathroom. Fifteen minutes later I was ready to deal with Ms. Vasquez and the world. I walked into the kitchen, poured myself some coffee and dialed Marta Vasquez's number.

"Ms. Vasquez, Leo Haggerty. I understand that you called me?"

"Yes. I was at our bank yesterday. I found out that Malcolm had looted our account. That asset was to be frozen until we'd made a property settlement. He'd closed it out and then opened one for himself at the same bank. But he didn't put all the money in the new account. Five hundred dollars was missing. When the police gave me his effects, his wallet had only thirty dollars in it. I want that money found."

"Hold on a minute. What did the bank say about the transaction?"

"They couldn't find the deposit slip yesterday. But they said that if I came down today, they'd show it to me. He either had them issue a bank check or took it in cash. If it was in cash then he was robbed, don't you see?"

"I see." He could also have opened an account elsewhere or spent it later that day. "Ms. Vasquez, when they turned over your husband's effects to you, was there anything unusual, a purchase he might have made, that would account for the missing money?"

"No. I recognized everything in his suitcase."

"Was there anything in the car?"

"I didn't look."

"Would you, please. Trunk, glove compartment, under the seats, behind the seats, ashtrays, spare tire well, above the visor." If it was hidden better than that we'd need Waldo the Wonder Dog to sniff it out. "When are you going to the bank?"

"I was going to go over as soon as it opened—at nine o'clock."

"Would you mind waiting for me? I'd like to talk to the bank people myself."

"Okay."

"I'll be there, say, nine-thirty. Where do you live?"

She gave me the address. Just as I was about to hang up, she said, "Oh, call Mr. Grossbart. He had something to tell you. I think it was the doctor's report."

"Okay. I'll see you in about thirty minutes."

Nate's courier banged on the front door. I got my contract and gave it to him. Then I picked up the phone to call Grossbart.

"Law offices."

"Nate Grossbart, please."

"Who shall I say is calling?"

"Leo Haggerty."

"Thank you."

Nate was on the line immediately. "The pathologist's report is ready, Leo."

"Nate, what pathologist's report are you talking about? The M.E.'s report isn't even ready yet."

"I know, I know. I decided not to wait for those schmucks to get around to it. Toxicology screens have to be done immediately if there are traces of poison in the system. So I hired a private pathologist, Harvey Bliss, to do the work right away. Here's his number, 555-0878, call him, listen to him."

"All right, Nate, I'll be in touch with you." I dialed Dr. Bliss's number.

"Bliss, Moeller and Wendkos."

"Dr. Bliss, please."

"Hold on."

"Harvey Bliss speaking."

"Hello, Dr. Bliss, my name is Leo Haggerty. Nate Grossbart said I should give you a call, that you'd done some toxicology screens on Malcolm Donnelly."

"Yes, that's right. Hold on, let me get the report."

I doodled a note to myself to remember to ask Marta Vasquez about her husband's car.

"Okay. In a nutshell this is it. The preliminary report from the M.E. was on the money. Malcolm Donnelly died of respiratory failure brought on by the interaction between alcohol and a meprobamate compound. Time of death was between five and six P.M."

"You said interaction, not overdose?"

"That's correct. The blood levels on the drug were under three milligrams per, so he didn't take too much of the drug. But its interaction effects with alcohol are quite powerful. Only a little bit of the drug in his system, and only a little bit of alcohol I might add, are necessary to precipitate a coma and respiratory arrest."

"Would this be a rapid sequence of events?"

"Yes, most likely."

"What kind of drug would this compound be?"

"It's an antianxiety or antidepressant medication."

"Both?"

"Well, it's used with certain depressed patients who are extremely agitated."

"Who would prescribe such a medication?"

"Psychiatrists, internists, general practitioners, usually. I doubt that it was prescribed, though. The amount in his system was not a therapeutic dosage. He didn't have enough in his system to do him any good."

"But just enough to kill him, right?"

"That's right."

"Thank you, doctor. Is there anything else?"

"No, that's it."

I kept doodling on my notepad. Five hundred dollars? Time from bank to Grossbart to hotel? Maids? Sproul? Medical history?

Chapter 9

MARTA VASQUEZ LIVED in an older residential section of northwest Washington. The house was a red brick box with a screened-in side porch. I knocked on the door and was greeted by her in a black silk dress, a little short and slinky for mourning. She waved for me to enter. "Be right with you, Mr. Haggerty."

In the kitchen were two small children, a boy and a girl. They looked about eight and six. Behind them was the brown expanse of their babysitter, an older woman with the broad facial planes of an Indian. Ms. Vasquez returned with a short coat, beret and gloves. She knelt before the children and spoke to them in Spanish. A kiss and hug for each child, some last-minute instructions for the sitter and we walked out.

"Excuse me, did you check your husband's car?"

"Yes. I didn't find anything."

"Mind if I look at it? There are some other places I thought to check." Not that I don't trust you.

"Of course. That's it over there." She pointed to a Toyota sedan. I took the keys she handed to me and checked under the hood, the bottom of the chassis and all the places I'd mentioned to her. They were clean. I gave her back the keys.

I opened my car door for her and admired her legs as she slid into place. Driving to the bank she tapped out a Winston and lit it with a slim gold lighter. Blowing the smoke out her partly opened window, she said, "You don't like me much, do you?"

"That's not what you hired me for."

Another long pull. "No, not really, I guess. I just want you to understand that I'm not just out for the money. Of course I'm sorry he's dead. But I didn't love the man at the end and I couldn't live with him any longer. The gonorrhea was the last straw."

"Where were you when your husband died?" In your face as we used to say on the playgrounds of Riggs Park.

"What?" She recoiled.

"Look, Ms. Vasquez, you've raised the possibility of a robbery and maybe even murder. As far as I can see you've got a two-hundred-thousand-dollar profit margin on his death and no special fondness to see him avoid that end. As a suspect you glow in the dark. Let's skip over motive and go to opportunity. You are my client. Tell me you were delivering a televised press conference at the time of death. I'll sleep easier."

Her lips were white from pressure and her eyes a shade blacker. "Okay. Fine. I left Mr. Grossbart's office about three o'clock. He said I shouldn't let Malcom have the children. So I drove straight home and picked the kids up from school. You can check on that. I had to sign in at the school office. They played next door until about five-thirty. I finished cleaning up and cooked dinner. We ate about six. I gave them baths. Duncan had some homework. I read to the children and put them to bed at eight-thirty." She stared at me. "Do you want me to go on?"

"Yes."

"Okay. I made myself a drink and called my sister Christina — no, it was a local call, and told her what was going on. I watched a little television, tried to read, had another drink and fell asleep about ten-thirty. I woke up about three-thirty, I just couldn't sleep. So I went in and took a shower, and cried some. The kids couldn't hear me over the water. I got dressed and sat waiting for the paper to come. I had coffee and read the paper. At seven-thirty the kids were up. I made them a nice breakfast — eggs, sausage, toast. They sat down to cartoons around nine. I went back to bed. I guess I was depressed by what Malcolm had said he'd do. Around lunch the police at the door woke me up. That's when I found out about Malcolm. Believe me, everything about that day is engraved on my mind."

Perhaps, I thought, but my mother taught me not to believe anything I heard and only half of what I saw, and she was hell on my alibis.

"Did the paperboy see you?"

"No. I waited until he was out of sight to step out and pick up the paper."

Not bad for an impromptu alibi. I'd test it later on.

"I know it's not great, but I wasn't planning to have to need an alibi."

I glanced over at her. She still had her arms across her lap and the cigarette dangled sullenly from her red lips. "Nate said your husband was charging that you were an unfit mother. What did he mean by that?"

"I have no idea. The man was insane. He was raving. I was—what am I saying—I *am* an excellent mother. After all, that's what he wanted. A mother for his children, a cook and maid and cheering section, all rolled into one."

"What about you? What did you want?"

"I wanted a way out. I wanted to leave Argentina. I wanted to be free, to be safe. No more disappeared ones. A handsome military attaché was as good a way out as any. I was not unattractive and I made myself available. It was a good deal all around."

"What happened?"

"What indeed. It was not that cold-blooded a thing at the beginning. We were in love or at least mutually inflamed. Malcolm was a dashing figure. We married and I left Argentina. Malcolm was rotated back to the state department here. For a while I guess things were okay. I loved being in this country. It was all so new. I loved Malcolm. I was grateful. I got pregnant. I took care of the children. But slowly I started to realize Malcolm wasn't really here very much anymore. He was quite ambitious, you know, and he was always working, always hustling. I was supposed to raise perfect children, throw perfect parties, look perfect on his arm at receptions and never complain. After all, he had liberated me. It wasn't enough after a while. He didn't get promoted fast enough and then not at all. He was frustrated. Anything that I did or the children did that he didn't like, he blew up, screamed and yelled. Duncan began to wet his pants again. Heather started sucking her thumb. I began to hate him. It just went downhill. He drank more and more. We stopped sleeping together. I wanted to get into therapy, but he said never, it would mess up his security clearance. That told me where I stood."

She put her hand to her forehead and rested her elbow on the window edge. "I must have loved him somewhere, sometime, because it hurt so bad being shut out of his life. I really did want all of him, the good and the bad, like you vow. But I just couldn't go on getting so little. His last little present was the end. I told him to leave. He refused. I called some friends who were divorced. I admit I wanted to hurt Malcolm every way I could. Nathan Grossbart came well recommended. He told me not to move out, that it would look like desertion. He said I should try to force Malcolm to leave. He wouldn't. He said he'd get into therapy. I told him it was too late. I don't think he wanted to change anything but my mind. A messy divorce can't be good for your security clearance, can it?"

"In Nate's office you mentioned debts."

"Oh yes. Malcolm had complete control of our money. I mean he was the one who earned it, right? All I got was money to run the house. The only way I could get some decent clothes was to complain that I wouldn't look nice at some embassy party. He kept telling me he was putting money away in savings for the children, for us to retire on. Ha! He spent every penny he made and had huge credit card bills. He charged all kinds of things. He was entertaining god knows who on his own, trying to move up the ladder. We had bills due to all kinds of clubs he'd joined. I looked at the bills last night. I owe almost fifty thousand dollars. And we have almost nothing in the bank — no savings, no investments. He even took out the equity in the house and spent that. So there I am with the kids, what, a secretary maybe, in an apartment and owing that money for Malcolm and whatever he was pursuing. No, there's two-hundred-thousand dollars due me, thank you. I don't intend to let it pass me by without a fight." She exhaled slowly and turned to face me. "And I've hired you to fight for me."

"That you have."

"How well do you fight for people you don't like?" She leaned back against the door frame. I could imagine Malcolm Donnelly on a Buenos Aires balcony with her. Looking into those dreamy eyes, tasting that full-lipped mouth and being in deep water real fast. A riptide in the blood.

"Ms. Vasquez, I don't like your attorney and some of that spilled over to you. I figured you for one of those women that hires Nate to take no prisoners. Now I'm not so sure. You made your husband sound like a real viper but you also threw some mud at yourself. I like that. You'll get my best effort, just like any other client, because I do a job right or I don't do it at all."

The bank was coming up on our left. I parked the car and followed her into the bank. I'd heard it said that banks had drive-in windows installed so that cars could get to meet their owners. The manager, an anorectic plank of a woman as hard and severe as a two-by-four, checked Marta's signature card and other identification. After she signed some papers the manager slid her a copy of her husband's last act of betrayal. She looked at it for a moment and slid it over to me. Malcolm Donnelly had opened an account in his name only. Then he wrote a check for thirteen hundred dollars from their joint account and deposited eight hundred into his new one. The remaining five hundred he took with him.

"Do you know who handled this transaction?" I asked.

"I did," the manager said. She folded her hands in front of her, banished her smile and became a fortress of rectitude.

"Did he take the money in cash or did he get a bank check?"

"He took it in cash."

"Do you remember how?"

"Five hundreds as I recall." Big bills. Hard to break. Don't spend it all in one place, my mother used to say.

"Do you remember when he came in to do this?"

"It was right at two. He was the last person in the bank. I had to unlock the doors to let him out. He left at about two-fifteen."

"Do you remember anything unusual about him?"

"He was in quite a hurry. He ran to get inside before we locked up. He looked very impatient while I checked the account balance since he was closing it out. He didn't even bother to order checks. He just got up when I finished counting out his money and went to the doors. I had to hurry to open them for him. He didn't take his deposit slip or depositor's contract. We would have mailed the copies to him, of course."

"May I see the contract, please?" I asked.

She turned her gaze to Marta who said, "It's all right." The manager swiveled behind her desk, pulled open a drawer, found it and slapped it on the desk. I looked at it and asked if we could keep the depositor's copy. She shrugged yes, and I peeled it free. After refiling the document she looked up and said, "Is there anything else?"

"No, thank you. You've been quite helpful."

I steered Marta Vasquez to the door and then into the car. As I turned the engine over I handed her the contract. "By the way, I believe you. Your husband didn't intend to die that afternoon."

She let out a sigh and began to rummage in her purse for another cigarette. "What made you decide to believe me?"

"That." I flicked the corner of the contract. "Read it."

Her eyes scanned the page. She flipped it over and read the back. "But there's nothing there."

"Exactly. It's what isn't there that interests me. There's no beneficiary named in the death clause. Not you, not the kids whom he swore he'd never let you keep, not a secret girlfriend, nobody. Malcolm Donnelly was in a hurry but not to die."

"What do we do next?" She was smiling at me. It was

a magnetic smile, generating quite a pull. I thanked my stars she was a client and I had Samantha.

"What I do next is drive from here to Nate's office and time it, then time it from Nate's office to the hotel. I want to know if he had time to lose or give away that five hundred before he got to the hotel. I'll drop you back at your place first though."

"Fine."

We drove in silence back to the house. When she let herself out, she turned back and looked at me. "You know I loved him once, but it died somewhere along the way. I wanted out but I didn't want him dead. More than that, my kids didn't need him dead. Money or not, I want to find out how and why he died."

She turned to the house and walked away. A lady in black, in mourning for her own dead dreams. She'd been going through the mansion of her love, turning off a light in each room for each hurt she'd endured. One day she'd turned off the last light in the last room and everything was dark.

Chapter 10

AFTER I DROPPED Marta off at her house, I drove back to the bank and timed the drive from there to Nate Grossbart's office. It was fifteen minutes from the bank lot to Nate's front door. When I walked in his secretary was pouring over some chicken scratchings she had to decipher and type. She looked up when she heard the door close.

"Hello, Mr. Haggerty. Can I help you?"

"Last Friday, when Mr. Grossbart had his meeting with Marta Vasquez, what time did her husband come in here?"

"The meeting began at 2:30, I think." She flipped back to that date on Nate's daily log to check her memory. "Yes, here it is: 2:30 — Vasquez. Mr. Donnelly was here right after they started. He stormed past me, pushed open the office door and started yelling. I went to the door to see what Mr. Grossbart wanted me to do. He waved me back to my desk. He'd hit the intercom button on his phone, so I could take down everything he said. Mr. Donnelly was only here a couple of minutes, then he came back out. He slammed the doors hard enough to rattle the walls."

"Could I see your notes? I'm trying to pin down exactly what Mr. Donnelly's frame of mind was on that day."

"I guess so — you are working for Mr. Grossbart."

Don't remind me. She went to a records room down the hall and returned with the file. She slipped out a copy of the notes she'd made and handed them to me. They matched Nate's version of what Donnelly had said. Now I half believed him. I handed them back to her and said,

"Thanks. I'll be back a little after five to pick up my contract."

It was eighteen minutes to the hotel. The only way Malcolm Donnelly could have disposed of that five hundred bucks before he checked in was to throw it out his car window or eat it. Not very likely. I got a parking chit just like Donnelly's and walked up the lobby and asked to see Donnelly's room. After a short phone conference with the chief of security the deskman gave me the key. He also told me that the security chief wanted to see me in the lounge after I'd left the room.

I queasily took the glass-walled elevator up to the sixth floor, found the room and let myself in. Like Sproul had said, there were no signs of forced entry. The chair Donnelly was found in was facing me. I walked into the bathroom, stared out the window, walked back out and closed the door behind me. Finally, I slumped down in the chair Malcolm Donnelly died in and looked at his last sights. A double bed covered with a spread the color of beef stew. A copy of the D.C. innkeepers law and a DO NOT DISTURB sign on the back of the door. A low dresser and my own face above it in the mirror. The closed bathroom door was to my right.

I looked at myself in the mirror. Well, Malcolm, here's where it all came to a halt. What happened? You checked in here with a pint of gin, five hundred dollars in your wallet, a little bit of poison in your blood and a bellyful of hate. What happened? You didn't just sit here for a few hours doing nothing, then out of the blue write a suicide note, tuck it under the phone and hope you had enough poison in your system to die from. Malcolm, where'd the drugs come from? Where'd the note come from? Where'd the five hundred bucks go? I sat there wistfully looking into the mirror, waiting for my face to rearrange itself into Malcolm Donnelly's. Then he'd answer all my questions and tell me to go home to a woman who still had a light on for me.

I hoisted myself out of the chair and locked the door behind me. The chief of security was waiting for me in the lounge. He got up and held out his hand as I approached. I shook it. "Leo Haggerty," I said.

"Brian Rourke." Trippingly off the tongue. Twenty years a Boston cop I guessed. Here to get away from the cold. I had a feeling he'd been a good one. That pale, lumpy potato of a face would be real easy to underestimate. The bad haircut and jug ears didn't help any.

"I'm here investigating the death of Malcolm Donnelly."

"Who for?"

"The widow."

"You got some ID?"

I held out my license.

"So?" he said.

"So, could you tell me how the body was discovered?"

"That's all in the police report."

"Should have been. I'd like to hear it from you."

"Two of our girls, Roxanna and Camilla, opened the room because it was after checkout and Donnelly hadn't requested another day. They were going to get it ready for someone else. When they opened up the door and saw him sitting there dead as a doornail, they started screaming and ran down the hall and called me. I went up, took one look, closed the room up and called the police. That detective Sproul was the first one in the room."

"You're sure of that? The girls didn't go in the room?"

"Sure I'm sure. They went batshit, jabbering about zombies. Them Haitians are good workers but what a superstitious lot. Voodoo, hoodoo. The whole time we were standing there waiting for the officers to arrive, they were wailing and crying and crossing themselves. Something about the unblessed dead and it being bad luck to see one. Christ! They never did calm down. I had to send them home. They couldn't even look at the guy, much less go into the room."

"Did Donnelly have any guests?"

"No one who came to the desk asking for him."

"How many girls work this hotel?"

"Why do you ask?"

"Donnelly had five hundred dollars on him when he died. Sounds like he wanted to party."

"The hell you say. Sproul counted the money right there in front of me and his partner. The guy had thirty bucks on him."

"Okay. Maybe he had a visitor then. So how many girls work this place?" I scratched the maids and Sproul from my list of possible thieves.

Rourke shrugged. "Hard to say. Vice sends us mugshots. I see a familiar face, I boot her. Anyone obvious we move on. Unattended ladies in the bar have a thirty-minute time limit. Then I go introduce myself. If a girl hasn't made the books yet and she's tasteful she could work here six days a week and we'd never know it."

"Anybody working permanent nights on this beat?"

"Wisinski."

He would, I thought.

"Anything else?" Rourke slowly unwrapped a butterscotch lozenge and popped it into his mouth. I've seen hippos with better teeth.

"No. Thanks."

Rourke nodded and shambled to the lobby. I got up from the table, walked over to the bar and pulled up a stool. The bartender came over to take my order. I only wanted answers.

"The guy who died here last week, did any girls come in asking about it?"

"What's it to you?"

"Don't be an asshole. I asked a simple no-load question. If you can't answer it, I'd have to become suspicious. And I'd have to tell Rourke about my concerns. We don't want that, do we?"

"Nobody's come in here asking about it."

"There you go; that didn't hurt none, did it." I spun off the stool and went looking for the doorman.

Donnelly hadn't left his room to pick up a woman. So he'd let his fingers do the walking. She'd come in and gone straight to his room. If the whole five hundred was meant for her it would have been an all-nighter and a class act.

She'd have been dressed for success and cruised through the lobby like she owned the place. I stopped at the lobby phone and called Ms. Vasquez.

"Ms. Vasquez, this is Leo Haggerty. One question. Did your husband have an address book?"

"Yes."

"Is it there at the house? If so, could you go get it?"

"Sure. Hold on a minute."

I looked out at the street. The Fourteenth Street restoration was underway. The strip joints, topless bars, gay baths, model services and massage parlors were all gone now. Just a couple of adult movie houses and bookstores left. That and the hookers. Hooker: D.C.'s contribution to the lexicon of vice. During the civil war, General "Fighting Joe" Hooker was in charge of the defense of the capital city. The South never mounted a serious threat to the city, so his army squatted here and festered with boredom. Plenty of camp followers collected around Joe Hooker's bored soldiers. Eventually the army moved on. Hooker's women stayed put.

Marta Vasquez returned. "Got it."

"Okay. Go through it. Any name that you don't recognize but it's clearly male, I want you to call and find out who they are. Any name that's female or questionable or any number without a name I want you to give to me." While she went through the book I went back to surveying the streets. The number of working girls out there had tripled since they'd built the convention center. The "trickle-down" theory seems to work for sex at least.

"Sorry, there's nothing here like that."

"Okay. Thanks."

"Did you find something out?"

"No. Just an idea that I had. I'll let you know if it leads to anything."

Before I went out to see the doorman, I made sure that I was prepared to do business with him. He was in full dress with top hat and tails. Hands clasped behind his back he rocked back and forth. A car pulled into the driveway. He hurried to open doors, check whether bags needed to

be carried, summon bell captains with the briefest of nods
and smile a few welcoming words. I sidled up next to him
and began to rock in time with him. He didn't even grace
me with a sidelong glance. I rocked on. "Guy died here
last week," I said.

"So they say."

"Anybody show an interest in that fact?"

"You mean other than you?"

"Yes, other than me."

"And who would you be?"

"A friend of the family. They have an interest in his last
hours."

"I see. Well, I have friends and a family too."

"I can appreciate that. Perhaps I can interest you in an
idea that I have."

I took his silence for interest and began. "I have this idea
that the man in that room invited a young lady up to have
some fun. Well, she went up and he had this heart attack
and died, see. She got frightened and ran away. Maybe
she was afraid that someone had seen her and that people
might be looking to ask her a lot of questions. So she
watched and waited but there was nothing in the papers
or on T.V. about it. She got kind of worried. Maybe she
works this hotel a lot and needs to come back here. So she
shows up one day and asks around. She asks a friend maybe
what the story is on the dead guy. He tells her it's gone
down as a suicide and not to sweat it because nobody's
been asking about her. So she says thanks to her friend and
relaxes, 'cause there's nothing to worry about."

"Interesting story."

"Yeah, ain't it. But is it true? That's all I want to know."

"What do you think?" he said.

"Oh, I like it as stories go. The family would like to
believe it, too. The cops have closed the book on this one.
Nobody wants to make any trouble — but you know, a guy
dies, the family wants to know for sure how it happened
so they can bury their doubts with him. What do you say?"

"Well, I'll have to ask my associates."

"Of course. Who do you represent?"

"The Jackson brothers, all three of them."

"A well-known family, but wasn't there a death recently? I hear there's only two brothers left."

He rocked on. First he pursed his lips, then he furrowed his brow, finally he said, "You may be right. Fact is, as I think about it, you are right."

"Fine. Give me a name and a description and we'll shake on it."

"A deal, my man."

I reached into my pocket and palmed the two prefolded twenties. The doorman and I shook hands.

"Girl's name is Fancy, that's all I know." His eyebrows rose in the hope that I was a total moron. I squeezed his hand harder.

"One more like that and you'll have a permanently green palm. Understand?"

"Absolutely, brother."

I kept squeezing. "One more time, now. A description and her pimp's name."

"Okay, okay. She's a slope. A chink maybe, who knows? Little bitty thing, maybe five feet, black hair down to her ass, calls everybody 'man,' got this gold front tooth."

"She work this hotel often?"

"Nah, that's why I remember her. Strictly street trade. Hard-working girl. A big earner."

"Who's her pimp?"

"Sorry, I couldn't hear you."

"Right." I had enough. Wisinski could fill in the blanks. I released my grip and walked away.

It was a little before one and I had to be in Georgetown by five to see Nate. Since traffic would begin to clog up by three, there wasn't enough time to go home or to the club to work out. I decided to get a bite of lunch, knock around downtown for a while, then drop in on Nate.

I drove up to one of my favorite restaurants. There's no ambience to speak of, the menu is largely irrelevant since it lists dishes they've never served and the service is strictly functional. The decor is of the checked oilcloth, candle-in-the-bottle variety, encased in high-gloss walls so red you think you're eating inside a fire alarm. But the food overcomes it all. Huge servings of robustly flavored southern Italian food. My kind of place. Nouvelle cuisine unnerves me. I'm uncomfortable around food I want to clap for.

I walked in, took a seat and the waiter came up, dropped a glass of water on the table, plopped down the silverware and began to recite the daily specials.

"Okay. I'll have the white pizza, the osso bucco and a carafe of the house wine."

He turned and walked away. When he pushed open the kitchen door you could hear the cooks screaming at each other. The two guys eating in the corner didn't even look up. Regulars.

I flipped out my notebook and made some notes. I had some phone calls to make. Maybe I could save some legwork that way. I fooled around with a scenario involving Mr. and Mrs. Donnelly. He calls her from the hotel. Tells her he wants to see her, talk to her. She's desperate, terrified of his threats. She goes to see him. He lets her in. They talk. She slips the drug in his drink. He dies. She leaves the note to cover her tracks, tidies up and splits. Later, Nate tells her she's out the two hundred grand. A technicality. If they can prove accident they get the money. Proving murder would be doing too good a job. I wrote down some more questions. It would work. I'd find out if it had.

My food arrived and I worked my way through it. I saved some of the pizza to spread with the veal marrow. When I finished, I paid up. It was quite reasonable for the quality of the food. My next quest was for a phone booth. There was one right across the street. I wanted to call a friend of mine, a private investigator who'd worked these same streets not so long ago. Maybe he could give me a lead on Fancy or her pimp. The phone rang once before he answered.

"This is John Rankin. I can't come to the phone right now. Please leave your name, telephone number, the time and date of your call and I'll get back to you as soon as

I can. Begin speaking after the beep. The tape will stay with you as long as you want to talk."

"John, this is Leo Haggerty. I don't care what she looks like or what she's doing to you, if you're there, pick up the phone." Nothing. "Okay, be like that. I'll be in most of this evening. Call me when you can. Take it easy."

I called Arnie next. No answer. Then Marta Vasquez. Ditto. I called Horace Wisinski's district house. He wasn't there but he was on duty midnight to eight.

I still had some time to kill before dropping in on Nate, so I thought I'd indulge myself with a movie. I drove back towards Georgetown and parked near a theatre that specialized in film festival series. The films of Australia was the current program. I looked at the schedule and my watch. *Road Warrior* was the offering. I bought a ticket and walked into the already darkened theatre. Two white-knuckled, goggle-eyed hours later I stood with Max staring at the sand leaking out of the overturned tanker, stunned but wanting to laugh. Out there alone, in the middle of nowhere, he'd done it all. He'd totalled the vermin. For a truckful of sand. The homesteaders were long gone, hauling the petrol north. Crafty bastards. Walking out of the theatre I couldn't shake the feeling that what I'd seen was a documentary.

Nate's office wasn't far away, and it was about time to go see him. I started to cross the street when behind me I heard a voice say, "Get out of the way, you honky asshole."

I turned around to see a bullet-headed black man standing there with his hands on his hips. Dapper, pencil-thin mustache, about five-foot five. Behind him stood a big white guy. With his long neck, pinhead and big eyes, he looked like an ostrich. Bringing up the rear, an even bigger black guy was cleaning his nails.

"Fuck you, nigger. Who do you think you are, Marvin Hagler?"

"If I was you'd be just another great white heap. Now move it before I hurt you some."

"Go around me. There's plenty of room in the gutter."

"Have it your way." He laughed. "Just one question. Where do you want the body sent?"

"You're a cocky little fuck, ain't you, Rev?"

"What it is, Leo." The Reverend Shafrath Brown stuck out his hand. We executed a modest street handshake taking into consideration my ethnic handicap. The Rev pointed to his white companion. "You know Mickey the Shark?"

"Sure. The loan arranger." There was something odd about his posture. Standing there splay-footed with his wide shoulders held back, he managed the rare feat of being big and bulky and looking dainty.

"Say it ain't so, Rev. You aren't working for this maggot farm?"

"No. Mickey had a memory lapse. Forgot a court date. We're helping him remember that the ACE Bonding Company never forgets."

"I can't believe this, Mickey. All that vigorish and you couldn't go your own bond?"

The Rev laughed. "Couldn't rightly. See, he's down there trying to convince the IRS that he's unemployed and ain't got no money at all."

"Where are the Pfeiffer twins?"

"Wardell tied them to the toilet." The big black guy grinned.

"You need better help, Mickey."

"What you doin' down here, Leo? The suburbs is your turf."

"Looking for a working girl—Asian chick, calls herself Fancy. You know her?"

"No. But if she's a slant, odds are she's on Eldorado Jack's string. That's all he runs. Likes that horizontal pussy. Speaking of Asians, is Arnie available? Got some work for him over in Little Saigon."

"Yeah, he's free. Where do I find Eldorado Jack?"

"You don't want to."

"Why not?"

"Even for a white boy he's crazy. A real gorilla pimp. Breaks his girls in with a cattle prod and wet sheets. I hear he's got a cage in his house for the ones that cross him. They'll do anything to stay out of that cage. Tell you true though, he ever puts a sister in that box, I send Wardell down to do some missionary work on his head, believe it."

"What's he look like?"

"Tall skinny dude, big Adam's apple. Calls everybody Jack. That and his goddamn Eldorado, that's how he got his name. Loves that car more than his girls, that's for sure. Mink seats, bar, T.V. — you name it, it's got it. Parks that sucker down near H Street and shoots the shit all night."

"He'll be there tonight?"

"I expect so." The Rev shrugged.

"Thanks, Rev. You and Wardell take it easy." I started to walk away.

"Haggerty, one last thing." The Rev wasn't smiling.

"Yeah?"

"He carries an Arkansas Toothpick big enough to surf on. Ain't bashful with it either. You cross that fucker, put him to sleep, cause he'll do you like that — " He finger-popped a period to the warning.

"Thanks."

Nate's office was five minutes away. When I walked in the receptionist handed me an envelope. My contract and the retainer check were inside. "Is Nate in?"

"No, he just left."

"Is his secretary in?"

"Yes."

I walked back to Nate's office. The secretary was still at her desk.

"Excuse me. Could you do me a favor? I need something from the Vasquez/Donnelly file. Nate said you'd know where it was."

"What was that?"

"The asset search Carmine did for him. I need to check it against something I found in Donnelly's bank account."

"Sure. No problem. I'll get it for you." She walked back to the file, slipped the item out, came back and handed it to me.

I scanned the list. As I'd guessed, Carmine had done

this about a week ago. The insurance policy wasn't listed. She hadn't been thinking about inheritance at that point. Still it could have been an impromptu thing. Marta Vasquez stayed on the list. I thanked the secretary and went out to join the homebound herd. The drive home seemed to take forever. Every time we came to a halt a moment of claustrophobia passed over me. Especially at interchanges.

Chapter 11

THE FIRST THING I did when I got home was to call my answering service and see if I had any messages. Samantha had called. Finally. Maybe the rewrite was done and she'd be back among the living. I rang her up and got her answering machine. That wasn't a good sign. Samantha used her machine to keep the world away when she was writing. I wasn't sure whether she ever listened to the messages she'd collected or just threw the tape away when it was full and then inserted a fresh one. Either way, when I heard her machine go on I usually just hung up, as I was about to do when I heard her say, "Hold on. Let me shut this thing off." I waited for the whirring to stop.

"Hi, Samantha. I got a message that you called."

"Yeah. It's done, over with, gone. I express mailed it to New York this afternoon."

"Are you happy with it?"

"Yeah, I am. I think it's the best work I've done, but then I always think that right after I've sent it off. The doubts set in in about a week. But enough of that, I want to see you, that's why I called. It's been almost forty-eight hours and I'm going into withdrawal."

"There, there. I told you I'd grow on you. It's taken more than a year but sieges are like that. Do you have anything in mind?"

"How about dinner at Clyde's? I have to be over that way to pick up a tape of the interview I did on channel ten. And then . . ." she made her voice low and husky.

"Yes, go on."

"I'd rather not say."

"Spoilsport. Okay. I'll see you at Clyde's in, say, thirty minutes?"

"Fine. Look for me in the bar first."

"Will do."

While I changed, I turned on the small set in my bedroom to see if there was any news about the bombings. Out my bedroom window I watched the sun set. The clouds were low and dense as they coalesced. Underlit by the setting sun an inverted landscape appeared. A patch of yellow-green sky became a distant lake. Around it the clouds had become a receding salmon-hued desertscape. Perspective, unmoored by a subtle interplay of light and shadow had put me in Arizona staring across the Grand Canyon. Slowly a Virginia sunset reasserted itself. I stole a glance at the television set. Lieutenant Simmons was speaking. He looked tired and unhappy.

"We have received the first communication from the group claiming responsibility for the bombing of the Vietnam Veteran's Memorial. I'm going to read the text of the message we received.

"'Greetings to the American People. We, the Standing Committee on World Justice, will continue to remind you of your grievous atrocities committed around the world. For too long you have sought to undermine legitimate governments, have aided imperialist invaders and supported corrupt despots. This cannot and will not be tolerated any longer. America claims it has a government of the people, by the people and for the people. Therefore, we have indicted and found guilty the American people and will continue to strike directly at them until you change your ways. If your government is representative of your will, then you will pay directly for that government and its actions. Your leaders will be strictly immune from attack. If you wish to confer such safety on people who do not represent your true wishes, so be it. Decrees from the committee regarding the guidelines for American foreign policy will be forthcoming. If these decrees are not followed retribution will be swift and aimed at the people.'"

The anchorman cut in. "Thank you, Lieutenant Simmons. Here in the studio we have with us Dr. Vernon Atherton of the Center for the Study of Terrorism."

Dr. Atherton didn't look so hot either. He was unshaven and carried more bags under his eyes than a porter at a rest home. A slight tic in his left cheek said he had little energy left in reserve.

The anchorman began. "Dr. Atherton, we know you have been consulting with the state department. Can you tell us what the situation is?"

"All I can tell you is my opinion of the situation. The state department is still formulating its response to the terrorists. First, the most effective response to the threats of this group can only be implemented on the basis of accurate intelligence. We need to know who this group is and what they actually want. Hopefully, their so-called decrees will clarify this. We do know that they are a new group. They have not claimed responsibility for any prior terrorist actions. Obviously, they are extremely dangerous. The indiscriminate savagery of their bomb attack, which seemed to have been merely an 'attention-getter,' places them at the very apex of the violence continuum. Beyond that, anything I might say would be speculative and I am loath to provide their action with any further publicity."

"I appreciate that, Dr. Atherton, but these people won't go away just because we don't talk about them, and perhaps some things you might share with us could help reduce the almost palpable anxiety everyone feels."

Dr. Atherton's tic began to accelerate. "All right. However, let me emphasize that this is entirely speculative. It seems to me that certain kinds of terrorist groups can be ruled out. The scope of their domain, as reflected in their title, Standing Committee on World Justice, points away from a religious or nationalist group. These almost always proclaim their identity with great pride in their titles and communications. The language of the communiqué, the caricature of our constitution, points to the possibility that these terrorists are Americans, perhaps a resurrected faction of the Weather Underground or some other radical, disaffected youths, punishing us for what they see as our country's wrongs. The other likely composition of the group would be terrorists for hire in the service of another government. America has been relatively free from terrorism at home because our retaliation to any terrorism openly sponsored by a foreign government would be devastating. A foreign government could be covertly sponsoring this group. It is usually nihilist or anarchist groups that hire out this way. The religious fanatics or nationalist terrorists wouldn't do that because it would taint their motives. Purity, of course, is essential to them."

"What do you foresee as the state department position, Dr. Atherton?"

"They're going to have to tread a thin line, providing enough security to protect the people without destroying the openness of our society. The brutal reality is that freedom and security are inversely related. Too much or too little of either one could spark disturbances unseen in America for at least fifteen years. Of course, speedy apprehension of these terrorists would be the best solution."

"Is there any connection between this group and the freeway bombing in Los Angeles?"

"Not that I am aware of at this time. Believe me, these are not the last groups we will hear from. A new age has arrived in America. How dark an age it is remains to be seen —"

I turned off the set. Someone had decided to give us a history lesson. No taxation without representation. That was how we were born. Well, we had representation now and they had levied a tax in blood on all our heads.

Twenty minutes later I pulled into the lot at Clyde's, parked and trotted up the steps to the entrance. The hostess smiled. "One?"

"Yes. I'm just going to have a drink."

She pointed to the bar to her left and turned back to greet the next people coming in. I scanned the room and didn't see Samantha. A guy slid off the stool in the far corner, so I headed for it. I asked the bartender for an Irish, neat. As he put the drink in front of me, I saw her walking up the stairs. She squeezed between two men at the bar and picked up the drink she had left there. She hadn't seen me yet. I tried to imagine her as a woman I didn't know. This exercise never fails to yield a desire that hurts. The men clustered around her tried to imagine her as a woman they did know. I watched her reserved half smiles and nearly attentive gaze, one part of her searching for me. I looked at her large green eyes. There were the beginnings of some laugh lines at the corners. No one takes a flawless beauty seriously. We seem to need those tiny failures of muscle tone to find character in a woman's face. I plead guilty to that bias. A hand through her hair betrayed a few gray hairs resolutely undyed. Her glass was empty. I signalled to the bartender and said, "Send a Virginia Gentleman and water to the woman over there." He was everything I wanted in a mixologist: prompt.

I watched as he slid the drink towards her. She looked up, startled. He bent forward and nodded towards me. She picked up her glass. I raised mine and mouthed, "Cheers." She excused herself from the men around her. They stared at me for an instant. Eat your hearts out, guys. I was surprised that my adolescent rage and envy was still there. The eternal outsider looking at the in crowd. They were slick, poised and polished, cut from a pattern I'd never fit. That's okay. Quasimodo gets the homecoming queen anyway. Do we ever grow up or just older? It wasn't just nice that Samantha was beautiful. She had to be. How else does the hunchback turn the tables? I thought I'd keep this truth to myself. Maybe I'd outgrow it yet.

Samantha came up next to me and put her arm through mine. "Howdy, stranger. Thanks for the drink."

"Shucks, ma'am, my pleasure. Would you care to share a bite to eat?"

"Actually, stranger, I had something a little more intimate in mind." She leaned herself against me and liquified my spine.

"Easy. Let's eat and talk first. It's been a couple of busy days."

"Okay."

I caught the hostess's eye and signalled two for dinner. She nodded and we followed her through the main dining room to a table near the palms that grew in the center. We sat and took the proffered menus. The hostess left and was replaced by a busboy with glasses of water. After a couple of minutes scanning the menu we were ready to order. A waiter appeared simultaneously with our resolve and took the good news to the kitchen.

Samantha leaned forward and rested her chin on her folded hands. I took a sip of my water. She licked her lips.

"You can't be serious, can you?"

"Nope." She was smiling as she shook her head.

"Post-rewrite mania, is that the diagnosis?"

"Afraid so." Samantha straightened up and folded her hands in her lap. "I'll try to do better. It's just that I've got this burden off me. I feel free, I want to play and I want you as a playmate."

"Sorry I'm not feeling playful right now. The fact is that after we eat I'm going to have to go back to work."

"No. Really? Why didn't you tell me when you called me on the phone?"

"Because I wanted to see you. I know how you get after a book is done. I didn't want you to go off and play by yourself if I wasn't free." A long pull on my drink didn't quench a thing. "I've missed you, that's all."

Samantha pursed her lips and nodded her head. "I've missed you too. That's part of why I'm so up. My work is behind me and I want to be with you, to enjoy you. I guess we're just on different shifts. What do you have to do?"

"I want to go see Arnie and then I have to go downtown to follow up a lead on this case I've got."

"Does it have to be tonight?" Samantha managed to ask that without whining.

"The people I'm looking for only come out after dark. The sooner I do this the better."

The waiter reappeared with our dinners and conversation ceased until he'd set out all the dishes and left. Between bites Samantha asked me about Arnie.

"I don't know what's going on with him. The next day we had practice at the dojo. He damn near killed me trying to teach me some stupid ass lesson in strategy that I can't even remember now. I've cooled down enough now to go see him and try to sort out what happened. I think the wall got to him. I don't know."

"Do you want me to come along?"

"No, thanks. This is just between him and me. After I get a reading on him I'll let you know if he's up to talking to you."

"Okay."

We finished our meals and I settled up with the house. Out in the parking lot I asked Samantha where her car was.

"Over on the station's lot. You don't have to drop me off. This place is well lit and there's lots of people around."

"You sure?"

"Yes, I'm sure. And besides I want you to get your work done so we can play."

"Will I see you tomorrow?" I asked more wistfully than I wanted to.

"Bet on it."

We kissed and I watched her stride off into the darkness, whistling a tune that I couldn't quite place.

Chapter 12

IN THE CAR I had doubts about dropping in on Arnie. I decided to tell him that I'd come by because the Rev had some work for him, and let it go from there. The house was dark as I approached it, but Arnies's car was in the driveway. That wasn't unusual. He often meditated in the dark. I knocked on the door. No answer. I took out one of my cards, wrote the information about the Rev on the back and stuck it in the door frame. As I turned to go I thought I heard something. The television. Now, that was odd. I knocked again, louder. No answer. Time to go around to the back door and take a look.

In the light from the television screen I saw Arnie's outline, sprawled in a lawn chair with crushed beer cans piled around him. The door was unlocked. Three strikes and you're out of character. I stepped into the living room.

"Yo, Arnie. How ya' doin'. Thought I'd drop by."

He lifted his head up off his chest. In the dim light you could see the shiny crosshatch of scars on his face and scalp. "Well, if it isn't my friend." He took another swig of beer. "You and your bright fucking ideas. Let's go down to the wall. Pay our respects." Another swig. "I went back to the wall last night. I couldn't stay away. I just kept staring at all them names. After a while I could swear I heard 'em calling me, asking me why I was over there. It ain't fair. We shoulda all come back. Better men than me died over there." He stopped and wiped his face with the back of his sleeve. "Shit, man, we were beautiful. We could do it all. You name it. We had heart, let me tell you. We did every damn thing they asked us to. We never backed up. They just never let us win. Do you understand that?" He hiccupped. "All those fuckers had was patience and endurance. So what did we do? We tried to wear them out. Jesus Christ, where were they gonna go? They lived there. Grandpa fought the French in the same valleys. They cut our fuckin' hearts out there. They bled us dry." Arnie's hands were fists he rammed against his knees like pistons to keep his eyes closed. Sorrow leaked around them. "Get outta here, while you still can. Fuck you all." He sprang up from the chair and slung it away from him. I took the hint and left.

In the car I tried to figure out how to help Arnie but I got nowhere with it. I kept seeing him walking to that wall, late at night. Looking at all the names. Looking for his own name. Hearing his buddies call out, maybe he'd even see their hands reaching for him. Maybe the wall began to look like a door. I'd heard of guys pulling out a .45 caliber ticket home, putting it up against their head, leaning back against the cool granite wall, feeling the hands of the dead welcoming them, saying "Wait up guys, I'm coming" and then sliding down that doorway, their brains flecking the names of friends gone too far, gone too soon. It seems to me that the names of every Vietnam vet who kills himself ought to go on that wall. They may not have died "in country" but the country was still in them.

Chapter 13

THIRTY MINUTES LATER I stepped out onto the Fourteenth Street corridor. If the city council wanted to be civic minded they'd give the corridor to the developers and have them build a four star brothel at one end. Lust, like rage, is ineradicable. You don't "clean up" combat zones, you relocate them. Seventy-five years ago a nationwide epidemic of righteousness closed all the houses of ill repute and dumped the girls out on the streets. The net result was the creation of a new urban predator: the pimp.

The corridor was warming up. The movie houses and bookstores had all plugged in their blinking neon grins. You can tell the players and their games by how they use their eyes. The hookers are trolling for the big trick. Their eyes brighten when a car slows down and then dim with sullen anger as it passes. Those just passing through look straight ahead or at their shoes. The voyeurs' eyes dart left and right, up and down but never meet another's. Look but don't touch. The "doers'" eyes scan, then lock on and track like fear-seeking missiles. Once on target they follow the mark, cut it from the herd and do him or her in an alley, hallway or parking lot.

Connections here are brief and precise. Girls and boys get into cars, out of cars, up doorways, down stairs, into alleys, on their knees, off their backs trying to make their quotas. Every now and then a pimpmobile would cruise by. The man checking on his employees. Pulling over to let one out and another one in. I hadn't seen a glitzed-up Eldorado yet. I'd seen damn few white pimps at all. I wandered through this scene looking for a long-haired Oriental girl named Fancy, a gorilla pimp named Eldorado Jack and a cop known as Hoss the Boss.

Eventually, I found Horace "Hoss the Boss" Wisinski. He was lounging against a car, chatting up a couple of pros. His leather sap gloves were in his belt, pinned there by his belly, and his hat was on backwards like a U-boat commander's. A chili dog with a full load of onions sank down his throat with all hands lost. I walked up to the Hoss. He put his hand on his chest, made an *O* with his mouth and let out a belch that would register on the radar over at National.

"Nice, Hoss. A class act."

He checked for any stragglers waiting to escape. Satisfied that he had purged himself, he leaned back against the car and turned to address me. His breath was a defoliant.

I waved at the invisible assailant. "What is this, ADW: breath?" I said.

He chuckled. "Keeps the streets clean. Nobody gets in my face. Want some?" He fished out a big wad of waxed paper from his pants pocket, unwrapped it and showed me a huge clove of garlic.

"I'll pass."

"Brenda roasts 'em and keeps 'em in olive oil for me. Hell of a girl." Brenda was his wife.

"I see you got a stripe back, Hoss."

"Yeah, they give 'em to me with Velcro now. Makes it easier to take 'em back. But you ain't here to do a documentary on my career. What brings you to this sewer?" As he asked that he lifted himself off the car and started his patrol.

"I'm looked for an Oriental hooker. Calls herself Fancy. Short, long—"

"Hair down to her butt. Real name Francine Ky, DOB 7-14-67. Three priors, no fixed address. Her pimp is Eldorado Jack."

"When did you get the microchip installed, Horace?"

"Just good police work, Hags. Got my own mug books.

Read 'em every day. Pays to do your homework. Ounce of prevention and all that shit."

"Have you seen Ms. Ky recently?"

"Nope. Her pimp'll show up pretty soon. She'll check in. You find Jack, you'll find her. This business or pleasure? I hear she's got a mixmaster for an ass."

"Strictly business. Tell me about Eldorado Jack."

"Ardis Parmenter, a.k.a. Eldorado Jack, a.k.a. who cares. Certifiable. Crazy about Asian chicks. A gorilla pimp, has them all terrorized. Lots of assault charges but they never get pressed. Brass 'nads, very macho boy. High profile in this town for a white pimp. Loves his little red wagon more than life itself. You want his priors and all that shit?"

"No. Where does he hang out?"

"He parks out front of that shitkicker bar, The Do-Si-Do, and holds court there."

"Thanks, Hoss."

"One thing, Hags."

"Yeah?" I turned back.

"You cross that boy and you better bury him. He's crazy and he'll keep coming back like crabs on a working girl. You hear me?"

"I hear you, Horace. Hang loose, my man." As I waved to him I saw his eyes flick across the street. A silver gray Mercedes with Maryland tags was cruising slowly up the street. A hooker was running up the street, looking back over her shoulder. The Mercedes stopped and two guys jumped out of the car, grabbed the girl by the arms and stuffed her into the car. Inside they started punching the hell out of her.

Horace began to pull on his gloves. "See you around, Hags. Duty calls." Horace flipped his hat around to the front and headed across the street. I watched his odd pigeon-toed gait, the arm and leg on each side moving together.

Horace ripped open the car door and started tossing bodies out. First the two guys, then the hooker. He rapped one guy with his nightstick, then grabbed the other two by their throats, pulled them up close to his face and bellowed, "Shut the fuck up, alla ya. You, outta the car, now." A third guy came out of the car. I walked across the street to see how this would turn out.

"Up against the wall, assholes, spread 'em and keep your mouths shut." That done, he quickly patted the four of them down. None of the boys looked old enough to vote. "What's going on here?" Horace asked.

One of the boys stepped away from the wall. "This, this . . ." he sputtered "woman, took our money and didn't do, uh, deliver, what we'd, uh . . . bought. We were just trying to get our money back."

Horace turned to the girl. "Officer, I don't know what they are talking about, honestly. " she said.

The kid tried to take a swipe at her. "You whore. You took a hundred dollars of ours and you only did. . . ."

The hooker pursed her lips and made kissing noises. The kid glared at Horace. "What are you going to do about this, officer? I want your badge number. My father's a lawyer. If you don't do something about this, we'll report you for dereliction of duty."

Horace pulled the kid up close and exhaled slowly. I winced. "I don't give a fuck if your old man's almighty God himself. What I'm gonna do, you snot-nosed little shit, is run your ass in on assault charges, abduction with intent to defile and soliciting. That's for starters. Try to explain that to poppa." At that, the hooker slid along the wall, kicked off her high heels and ran blindly across the street, barely avoiding being hit by a cherry red Caddy. Within seconds she was lost in the crowd.

"Look what you did . . ." the kid whined.

"No, you look what you did. You came down here to rent a stranger's mouth. You probably got what you paid for. Now go home. Clear offa my streets. Hopefully, all you got here was a good lesson." The three kids had regrouped, sullenly hanging their heads. "And anyway, for your information that girl's name is Robert." Two of the boys started snickering and pointing their fingers at Motormouth. He turned gray, lurched away and threw up on the wall of an X-rated movie house. Horace shook his head.

The three kids climbed back into their car and sped away. "Yuppie puppies. What a breed. Ankle biters, all of 'em," Horace said, then listened to his radio for a second. "Party time down the street. Gotta roll, Hags." I went back across the street in search of the red Cadillac.

Eldorado Jack was sitting in the backseat of his car. He had a woman on each side, one hand on a thigh, a drink in the other. Neither one was Fancy. Jack and the girls slid out of the car. He kissed his companions, patted their rumps and sent them back to work. I'd turned away from him and was staring at a window display of marital aids. In the window's reflection I took an inventory of Mr. Eldorado Jack Parmenter. Taller than me, rangy, long neck, big Adam's apple, sharp features, slicked back black hair, a manic light in the eyes. He had on a fortune in gold rings and chains. A flowered silk shirt was open to his navel. Snow in your veins will keep you warm these chilly nights. Lime green silk suit over purple boots, probably made from the hide of some endangered species. I watched him move around a bit. His clothes fit like a second skin and his crotch only lacked for a neon arrow. The toothpick would be in his boot or more likely under his arm.

I had company. A little Oriental girl had entwined her arm in mine. Close but no cigar. "What'cha looking for, honey?" She nodded her head at the window.

"Nothing."

"I can do you better, honey. Make you real happy." She stopped popping her gum and smiled. There wasn't enough juice in it to brighten a penlight.

"What's your name?" I asked.

"Toy. What's yours?" My toy was emaciated. Another teenybopper vein popper on the oblivion express.

"How about Joe? You know a girl named Fancy?"

My friend dropped my arm. "No."

I reached out for her. "She made me real happy. I want to see her again. Tell you what. You tell me where she is, I'll introduce you to a friend of mine — Mr. Grant." They learn to put a name to faces real fast. The streetwalker I.Q. test: name the presidents on American bills from one to a hundred. You have ten seconds, begin now.

She looked at Jack for an instant. He was slinging shit with another "man of leisure." "So, Jack," he said, "you know why a whore's like a cheap watch?" His eyes were boring into the other guy. Finger popping, he could barely wait to get to the punch line. Finally, he rapped his doltish companion in the chest. "They take a lickin' and keep on trickin'." I thought Jack would have a stroke he was so convulsed by his own wit.

"C'mon tell me. I'm no trouble." I took her by the arm and walked down the street with her. My other hand I slipped inside my jacket and showed her the fifty. She was as desperate as a hamster in its wheel. I wasn't real thrilled at lining Jack's pockets, but it would be the easiest fifty she'd make tonight. She might make quota and dodge a beating. I wasn't long on rescue fantasies. Sad but true, people do what they want to do. We can bring each other down but you can only lift yourself up.

"Yeah. I know Fancy. She's in deep trouble. Jack heard she's thinking of going outlaw on him. He's real angry."

"Is she hiding somewhere?"

"I don't know. Jack said he'd forgive her and not hurt her if she came out tonight. She has to bring him an offering. You know, a gift. Something for his car. He's waiting to see if she shows up."

"All right. Here." I gave her the bill and figured I'd sit on Mr. Eldorado Jack Parmenter like a buzzard and see what happened.

If you stand still on these streets people figure you've opened up a shop and they browse. A couple of leather boys sized me up. I moved my head no, like a pitcher shaking off a signal. They moved on. I wanted to be close enough to Jack to intercept this girl if she showed up, but not right in his lap. Ten minutes later I saw her. She was hurrying down the street with a package clutched to her chest. Jack hadn't seen her yet. I stepped out of the doorway I'd taken root in and walked right into her. She caromed off me and dropped her box. I picked it up. She was frantic to get it back.

"Give me that, man, it's mine. Please."

"No problem. I just want to talk with you for a second. Then you can be on your way."

"No way, man."

"Then I'll hold onto this, darling." She looked down the street to where Jack was. She was terror stricken. "Don't be afraid of Jack. If you don't want to talk to him or work for him, I'll help you. Just give me a minute. I just want to ask you one question. I'll pay you for your time, top dollar."

"Look man, I can't. If Jack sees me even talking to you, he'll think I'm cheating on him or trying to leave. He'll hurt me. You don't know him. He'll find me. Please give me my box. Please." I thought about holding on to the package and then feeding it to Jack. Instead I slipped out one of my cards and gave it to her. "This is my name and number. When you get a minute, call me. I just want to ask you a question. There's money in it and it won't get you in trouble. If you want to leave Jack, call me. I'll help you get out." She took the card and slipped it into her purse. I gave her the box. Jack pushed through a strolling couple, grabbed her by the shoulders and shook her.

"What you doing'? This your new man?" He turned toward me and undid the one button on his jacket.

I marked him as right-handed. I backed away, palms up. "Hey, easy. This lady just dropped her package. I picked it up and gave it back to her." Over Jack's shoulder I watched Fancy's eyes. She pulled on his arm.

"Jackie. Baby. Please. Fancy's back. Let me show you what I got, baby. Come on." She was climbing all over him, cooing, running her fingers through his hair. I backed off even further. Eldorado Jack watched me disappear into the crowd with the intensity of a man pinning a butterfly to a board. "Another time, my man. Another time." I muttered to myself. I backed into an immovable object and whirled.

"Easy, Hags. Easy. You're very tense, very tense." Hoss chuckled. "Saw that little display of discretion back there.

What they call the better part of valor, eh? Be patient. This guy's got a real knack for making enemies. You'll get a piece of him. Try not to do it on my streets, okay? I'm sworn to uphold the law and I do like peace and quiet."

"Wouldn't think of it, Hoss. Give my regards to Brenda." I'd had it with the circus. I found my car and left.

Chapter 14

SAMANTHA'S MUSTANG was in the driveway when I got home. I let myself in, walked back to the bedroom, pushed open the door and saw her in the clock's luminous glow. She was all curled up, one hip and leg draped over a pillow, her balled fist tucked close under her chin. Smiling, I sat down by the bed to get undressed. As I did that I thought of Marta Vasquez waiting in the dark for her husband to come back to her, and all the women we leave behind on our mad quests. I wonder how a Penelopiad would have told the story. Naked I slid in next to Samantha. She adjusted and then adhered herself to my shape. I kissed the nape of her neck and slid a protective arm around her.

When I awoke the bed was all mine. I wandered into the bathroom, cleaned up, slipped on a pair of shorts and went into the kitchen. Samantha had set out sun-dried tomatoes, cheese and muffins. Coffee was brewing. I went out to the driveway and retrieved the paper. I scanned the paper as I walked back to the house. Page one had the latest communiqué from the Standing Committee on World Justice. They demanded the immediate withdrawal of all our "forces of subversion" in Central America or there would be another summary execution of the "citizen sheep" of this country. A sidebar by Dr. Sumner Barfield, a colleague of Dr. Atherton, analyzed the rhetoric of the decree which equated Central America with Vietnam. Barfield noted that the anti-Vietnam activists had identified the government as the "enemy of the people," whereas this group had defined the enemy as the people. He concluded that this group was not a homegrown but rather an imported virus. Or words to that effect. Farther down I read that the final death toll in Los Angeles had reached 338 — the greatest number of people ever killed in a single terrorist attack anywhere. "There is no safety in numbers or in anything else." Thank you, James Thurber.

Samantha poured two cups of coffee and brought them with cream and sugar to the table. She took the front page and left me the sports page. The lead story was that many season ticket holders were expected to skip next Sunday's game. A bomb in the upper deck would collapse the roof overhang, killing thousands in their seats. I folded up the paper and put it aside. It was my turn to use the tickets.

Samantha flirted with me over the rim of her cup, wrinkling her nose, flicking her tongue over her teeth. All she wore was a T-shirt embossed with the marines logo and the words "Looking for a few good men."

"Hello, stranger," she said.

"Hello, yourself. It was nice finding you here when I came in." I sipped my coffee. "No, it was more than nice. It was perfect."

"I'm glad to hear that. How did your evening go?"

"Not bad. I made a fair bit of progress on this Vasquez case. Tell you something, though. I went by to see Arnie first. He was drunk as a skunk. He's really hurting too. He started to talk about it but then he threw me out. I've never seen him like that before. The walls may be coming down but I'll tell you I'm not sure what is going to be left standing."

"God, I'm sorry to hear that. Do you think I could talk to him maybe?"

"I don't know. You could try. He wasn't too happy to see me."

"What are you doing today?" she asked.

"I'm on hold on this case. There are a couple of long shot loose ends I could pursue, but that's it. If this witness I located last night doesn't come across on her own, I'll give her name to Nate Grossbart and see if he wants to drag her ass into court. Maybe we'll get somewhere that way. Otherwise I'm all yours."

"Hmmm. That's an interesting idea."

I got up to chase her around the table when the phone rang. After the fifth ring I was convinced it wouldn't go away, so I answered it.

"Sorry to interrupt your beauty sleep, Mr. Haggerty, but this is Sergeant Sproul. I'd like you to come down to Casualty Hospital. Got something to show you." After a second's pause he added, "You aren't going to make me come looking for you, are ya?"

"Wouldn't think of it." I hung up.

"Who was that?" Samantha asked.

"The cop on this case I've got says he has something to show me at Casualty Hospital."

"Do you have to go?"

"He was telling, not asking." I kissed her brow. "Besides, I'm curious."

"Can't I tempt you?"

"God yes, but please don't. I already don't want to leave. Don't make it any harder."

She frowned. "All right. If I can't keep you here I'll go with you." She slapped my thigh. "Let's go, Nick, you still have to walk Asta."

Fifteen minutes later we were on I-66 eastbound. Just before noon we pulled up to Casualty Hospital's emergency room entrance. An unmarked car complete with magnetic cherry on top was next to the sliding glass doors.

"Samantha, why don't you wait out here. This isn't a pretty place to be," I said as I got out of the car.

"Let me decide what I can handle. I'm not made of china, you know."

We passed under the electric eye and the doors silently parted and closed behind us. Casualty was well named. Ambulatory schizophrenics sat and conversed with their own private company as they waited for the paddy wagon ride to St. Elizabeth's. A young black man with a bloody compress over his right eye sat next to a woman who was squeezing and patting his hand. Sproul came around from behind the admitting desk.

"Come here, Haggerty."

Samantha moved to follow. He held up a palm. "Sorry, this is official police business. You'll have to wait here." She stepped back. We walked side by side down the corridor. Sproul was stale with sweat, rumpled and grim.

He pushed open a door. Inside a doctor stood by a bed. He turned to look at us. Beyond, I saw a figure. Most of its face was covered with bandages. There were tubes and lines running out of its arms.

Sproul introduced me with a wave of his arm. "Leo Haggerty. Francine Ky."

"Jesus Christ. What happened to her?"

"She won't say. We found your card on her. She'd been dumped in a trash can near Eighth and F. Beat cop found her about an hour ago and had her sent here. So what do you know?"

"I saw her on the street last night. She was going to see her pimp, Eldorado Jack. He was supposedly furious with her about going outlaw on him."

"Why'd she have your card?"

"I told her I'd help her get away from him if she wanted."

"Aren't you the noble one." Sproul snickered.

"Fuck you, Sproul."

"Touchy, touchy. What else?"

"I'd heard she was interested in the Donnelly death. I wanted to know why. She never said anything. So I left."

"Mr. Eldorado Jack probably didn't like your interest and decided to teach her a lesson." Sproul shook his head and looked ready to spit a gob of disgust.

"Have you picked him up yet?"

"Are you kidding? I don't have a complaint. This, this human punching bag"—he waved his hand to dismiss the whole scene—"is afraid he'll do even worse things to her. So she says she had an accident. His girls wouldn't pick him out of a lineup if he was the only one in it. I've got no complaint, Haggerty, so good-bye. I just thought you might have something we could use." Sproul turned and walked out.

The doctor pointed to the door. I went out with him. In the hall I grabbed his arm, a little too roughly. He looked at his arm with distaste. "Yes," he said.

"Sorry. I'm a little jacked up about this. What happened to her?"

"She said she slipped on a wet step and fell."

"Bullshit. You know what I mean."

The guy turned to face me and shoved his hands in his smock. "For starters he yanked out four of her teeth. Just repossessing the gold work, I guess. After that I'd say he used a vise grip on her. She'll never work again, not for him, not for anybody. You catch my meaning? Believe me, you don't want the details." He shook his head. "She isn't the first one of his we've seen in here. I'm sure she won't be the last."

I watched him walk away, checked the halls and let myself back into Francine Ky's room. I pulled a chair up next to the bed. Bandages covered her nose and an eye. Her other eye was closed. Her hair was tucked up in a net. I leaned close to her and whispered, "Francine, don't say anything. Just listen to me. You have my card. When you get out of here, I want you to call me. I'll see if I can help you out. Do you understand me?"

Nothing. Then a nod. "I want to ask you one question, that's all. Who asked you to go to the hotel and ask about Malcolm Donnelly? I just want the name and I'll leave you alone."

She still hadn't opened her eye. Her black, swollen tongue peeked out between her battered lips. I leaned closer to hear her, turning my head so that my ear was just above her mouth. "Don't know name." The words seeped out like bad air from a played out mine. She swallowed. "Cameron House, 3G."

I squeezed her arm. "Thanks. You call me when you're ready to get out." She turned her head away.

I left Francine Ky in that hospital room with nothing

but tubes and monitors for company. Samantha was sitting in the lobby. "What happened?"

"A girl I talked to out on the street got mutilated by her pimp. She's too scared to press charges against him. Probably with good reason. No witnesses. Her 'dubious moral stature' as they say. Jack'll get three other pimps to swear he was at a Bible class with them. He'd probably walk and if she were around he probably would give her a repeat performance. Fuck, who cares." I waved my hand at nothing.

I rammed a smile up my face. "However, Sherlock Haggerty did get a lead out of all this. That's what counts, right? She made her own bed, right? I'm just doing a job, right? Don't interrupt with an answer, Watson, I'm not in the mood." I hit the glass doors hard enough to shake the frame and stalked back to the car.

"What next?" she said as we pulled away from the hospital.

"I've got a lead to follow. I don't know where it's going to go."

"Okay. I guess my Nora Charles routine is over, huh?"

"Yeah. This is serious business and I don't want to be worrying about what you're doing or where you are."

"Why don't you drop me at a Metro stop? I'll catch a train home and get back to work." She hid her disappointment well, but not perfectly.

"All right."

"Will you be coming by tonight?" she asked.

"I don't know. Frankly I doubt it."

"Call if you know what your plans are going to be. I'll probably go over later to see Arnie. See how he's doing."

I let her out at the nearest stop. She leaned in through the window and blew me a kiss. "Are you okay?" she asked.

"Sure. Why do you ask?"

"Because I've seen that look before and it worries me. Don't do anything foolish."

"Don't worry. I'm learning my limits every day. 'Neither a hero nor a fool be.' Polonius's advice to Haggerty."

She shook her head. "Call."

"Go, you'll miss your train. I love you."

She pursed up her mouth, waved and went down the escalator to the platform.

Chapter 15

CAMERON HOUSE was a condominium on upper Connecticut Avenue. I punched 3G on the security system intercom. It buzzed like a fat spring fly hitting a screen door. One. Two. Three. Four. A sleep-thickened voice answered. "Hello."

"Hello, my name is Leo Haggerty—"

"We don't want any." She hung up.

I dialed again. Seven rings this time. "If you don't go away, I'll—"

"Call the police. Please do. They'll be very interested in talking to me. Don't bother with vice, go straight to homicide."

The voice got real clear. "Who are you?"

"I'm a private investigator. I'd like to ask you a couple of questions, very discreetly, since discretion is the soul of our professions, is it not?" I stared at the door while she weighed her options. I was buzzed in.

I knocked on 3G. There was a peephole. The door opened slowly on a thick chain. A hand reached around and a voice said, "Show me some I.D." I slipped my license out of my wallet and handed it to her. The door slammed closed. I looked at my watch. "Two minutes to check me out is all you have, darlin'," I said to the peephole.

Right on time the door was pulled open and I walked in. A woman in a terrycloth robe showed me in. One hand clutched the robe near her throat. With the other hand she gave me back my license.

I walked into the living room and took it all in. The white

walls were divided by a bold, plum-colored slash that wandered around the living room and then disappeared down the hall to the left. Gauzy, patterned curtains diffused the midday light. Three strange chairs sat around a large wooden coffee table.

One was an old throne chair with claw feet. The snarling heads of lions would be over the shoulders of the person who sat there. A loveseat was carved in the shape of a bleary-eyed old wino. One hand clutched a brown paper bag, the other was thrown over the back of a simple, straight-back seat that grew from his left hip. The third chair was an old bentwood rocker with a plum cushion.

To the left of the bedroom hallway was a game table with two chairs. Above it, a cabinet hung on the wall. To the right of the hallway stood a high-tech stereo system. Two Leonor Fini prints, at least I assumed they were prints, were on the other wall. Next to the picture window was a table with a computer system atop it. I guessed the kitchen to be off to the right.

The woman in the doorway had one of those all-purpose faces that most models have. All the right proportions and no glaring flaws. A face that could be enhanced by any new look, any new product without calling attention to itself. Good hit men have the same face.

Another woman walked into the room. They looked at each other for a moment, then the first one introduced herself.

"I'm Wanda Manlove. This is my apartment."

"Anita Coxworth," the other girl said.

"Of course, and I'm Luke Warm."

"Sorry to hear that," Wanda said.

"No doubt. I'd like to ask you a couple of questions about a man you met at the Presidential Arms last Friday."

"I don't know what you're talking about." She crossed her arms over her chest and gave me her best dead fish look.

"Cut the crap. Like I said, I have no interest in hassling you. Just answer a couple of questions and I'm gone. Otherwise, I call homicide and send them down here to rain on your parade. So what do you say? You talk and I walk?"

Wanda sat in the throne chair. I avoided my boozy wooden companion and took the rocker. She stared at me like I was a pimple on prom night. I glared back. In my mind I kept hearing Sister Benigna saying, "Your body is the temple of the holy spirit." Wanda, Wanda, Wanda, why'd you wanna make God a slumlord?

Wanda looked over my shoulder, then back at me. "All right, Anita says you're clean." The other woman was sitting in front of the computer console.

"Maybe we can compare databases someday," I said.

"I doubt it. How did you find me anyway?"

"A girl named Francine Ky gave me your name." A useful lie.

Anita and Wanda's eyes met for an instant. "When did you see Francine?"

"This morning."

"How's she doing?" Wanda tossed out the question like it was last year's look.

"Real poorly."

"Oh, that's too bad."

I thought she was going to yawn. I was getting tired of this charade. "Isn't it. Her pimp fucked her up so bad she'll never work again. Your name cost her plenty, so let's make it worthwhile and cut this bored, solicitous shit. I mentioned her name and this room got ten degrees cooler. What gives?"

"It's none of your business. What did she say?"

"She only gave me your name. I can fill in the rest, though. You asked her to see if there had been any inquiries about the guy who had died there, Malcolm Donnelly. She told you no, it was going down as a suicide and no one was looking for a woman who might have been in his room. But I know better. All I want to know is what happened in that room."

Wanda shook her head. "Shit. Where's Francine?"

"Over at Casualty Hospital."

"All right. I'll tell you what you want to know on one condition. Otherwise, I'll take the heat. It'll be an inconvenience but I won't do time for it."

"What's the condition?"

"You fix that animal pimp of hers. He's hurt enough girls." She pointed at me. "Look at that face. What's the matter, peeper? You've got principles? That's the deal, take it or leave it."

I sat there weighing my options. Out on the street and in that hospital room I had really wanted a piece of Jack. I wasn't ready to become a hired killer, though. For guidance I reviewed the two or three nuggets of enduring wisdom that had panned out after almost a dozen years of this work. I settled on Haggerty's Law of the Conservation of Effort: Never do more for somebody else than they're willing to do for themselves.

"Let's go, Mr. Private Eye. Is it a deal?"

"I'll tell you what I will do. I won't kill him but I will take him off the streets for a good long time. I'll do it tonight. But Francine Ky has to press charges after I take him down. You talk to her. Get back to me with an answer." I got up to leave.

"Wait a minute, how do we know you'll do it?"

"One of you can come along and watch if you want proof. Then call the other one and have Francine talk to the cops at the hospital."

"All right. You stay here though. I'm going to go down to the hospital right now and have a talk with her. I'll call here with an answer."

"Fine." I sat back down. Wanda stood up and went down the hall to get dressed. I leaned back and began to rock. Anita asked me if I wanted a cup of coffee. I said no. She, unlike her friend, was striking. Thick, lustrous black hair swept up from a pronounced widow's peak that gave her face almost a heart shape. The combination of large round eyes under the thinnest arch of an eyebrow, a Roman nose, and beestung lips gave her face a look of perpetual astonishment. All in a slightly olive cast.

Wanda returned, ready to go. I asked her why she was so interested in Francine Ky.

"She was supposed to meet us here today. She was ready

to leave her pimp, and we were going to help her learn how to work for herself."

"The word out on the street was that she was going to go outlaw and Jack knew it."

"Outlaw? Give me a break. Let me tell you something. I've never had a pimp and I never will. No son of a bitch is going to lie around, turn me out, work my ass to the bone, beat the shit out of me and take my money. Not in this life. What do I need one of those bastards for? To tell me he loves me? A pimp wouldn't know love if it ran up and bit him on the ass. The last few years I've made plenty. A couple more like it and I'm going to retire, and I'm not going to do anything I don't want to ever again."

"Is that what you were selling Francine?"

"Yes. Get her off the streets and away from that animal. We'd teach her how to manage herself. How to keep the money she earned. Get out of this rat race in one piece." Wanda picked up her purse and slung it over her shoulder. "Shit. I really thought we'd get her out. She was supposed to stay off the streets and away from Jack until she came here."

"Maybe she was trying to and Jack found out." The present for his car could have been a diversion, her desperation on the street because she felt that I was jeopardizing her escape. Then again, maybe not.

"What do you do, recruit the girls?"

"Yeah. One day a week, I go down to 'The Stroll' and look for someone with some fight in them. I take them out to lunch and make my pitch."

"Have any girls ever told their pimp what you're doing?"

"Not yet. I'm a pretty good judge of character."

"You'd better be. If the pimp's union ever gets onto you they'll toss you off Key Bridge."

"That's why I carry this." She pulled a little automatic out of her purse. "I keep a low profile, screen my clients very carefully and never trick where I live. I've been doing this for six years and I'm not on any police blotter anywhere. That guy dying though really put me on edge. I don't like that kind of visibility. So I asked Francine to check it out as a favor to me. When you showed up I thought cop or pimp, but the computer says otherwise. Anita's a real whiz with that thing." She dropped the gun back in her purse, put on a short coat and went to the door.

"One last thing though," I said, "the street law is very clear on this. Do unto others as they have done unto you. I'll keep my end of the bargain. You'll have a witness to that. If you don't keep your end of the deal I'll throw you off of Key Bridge. Understood?"

"Yeah, I understand."

When Wanda left, Anita asked me if I wanted something to eat. I said no thanks, but I would take her up on her prior offer of coffee. While she prepared a breakfast I went to the picture window and stared down at Connecticut Avenue. The zoo wasn't too far away and beyond that, off Columbia Road, was the city's Hispanic section, Adams-Morgan. Twenty years ago I'd lived there with a junkie from Texas named Bonnie Rasmussen. It was hard to accept that she loved the needle more than me. Maybe that was why I didn't leave after the first O.D. Maybe I thought that if I just loved her more, she'd give that stuff up. One day I walked in and saw her sitting there on the bed, naked, the needle in her arm, slowly pumping the junk into her arm and then letting it and her blood back into the syringe. Back and forth, back and forth she did that, all the while moaning in a way she never had with me. I went back to Bethesda. She moved in with her dealer.

"Here's your coffee," Anita said.

"Oh, thanks." I sat down at the dining room table with her and watched her work through some scrambled eggs and grilled ham. She wiped at her mouth and said, "Are you sure you don't want some of this?"

"No, that's okay."

"I guess I just feel odd eating in front of someone who's not having any."

"I'll go over and sit in the rocker."

"No, don't do that. Anyway I'm almost finished." She wiped her mouth with her napkin. "You and Wanda really hit it off big time."

"Right. I've got no beef with her. If everybody does what they say they will, we can help each other."

"I think it's real hard for her to need a man's help on anything."

"I just want her to know that asking me to take Jack down is serious business. I don't want her even thinking about fucking with me on this."

"Oh, I think your message came across loud and clear."

"Good. I hope she's as smart as she is tough."

Anita stood up and said, "Well, I've got work to do. Make yourself comfortable." She got up and walked down the hall.

While I sipped my coffee I considered my next moves. Marta Vasquez was still on the big board. Maybe what Wanda had to tell me would get her off. It would be a lot easier than taking a photograph of her and showing it around to the hotel staff. I yelled down the hall, "Do you mind if I use your phone?"

"No, go ahead."

I called the school board and by giving them Marta Vasquez's address I found out the name of her local school. The day-care program director had no qualms about answering my questions and yes, Marta had picked her children up that day. I thanked her and she told me that it was no problem — Mrs. Donnelly had said I'd probably call.

Anita came back out, dressed this time. She wore black stirrup pants and a pastel blouse with the sleeves rolled up. She sat down at the console and started to work.

"What do you keep in that thing?"

She smiled at me over her shoulder. "That's classified, sir."

"Of course. Silly me."

"We keep track of all our investments. That's what I do for Wanda and the other girls who want to invest their money. I keep track of things. Keep them posted. Make recommendations. Move money if they want to change investments."

"So you're the house broker?"

"You could say that."

"How'd you get started in this?"

"Hooking?"

"No, the investment end of things."

"I've always been real interested in money." She laughed. "It seemed to me that the trick was to let your money make money. Tricking was the fastest way to make good money, so I did that. I took some courses on investing and began to get the hang of it. The more my money started making me money, the less I had to trick. Wanda has lots of good ideas but she just doesn't have the temperament for investing. She wants everything right away. So she let me take over managing her assets and then the other girls'. I make most of my money from consultant fees these days. I still trick now and then. Just to keep my hand in. You never can tell what you'll need to do for money."

She turned back to her console and I went into the kitchen and poured out the dregs into the sink. The phone rang. Anita answered it and handed it to me.

"Haggerty, Francine will press charges against Jack, after we have word that he's been, shall we say, neutralized. Anita will go with you as an observer. I'll stay at home for the message. When she calls me to tell me it's been done, I'll go to the hospital and we'll call the police. Okay?"

"Fine. One thing. Don't tell any of Jack's girls about this. Believe me, the word will get out on the street about what happened. You can make your pitch the next day. I want Jack as fat and full of himself as he can be. Surprise is essential."

"Okay, no problem."

I hung up the phone and turned back to Anita. "I'll pick you up about six. Be down front. Our business should be over between nine and ten. Afterwards, you call Wanda. She'll be waiting here for your call. Then we'll all meet at the hospital for a little talk."

"All right. I'll see you at six."

Chapter 16

I DROVE HOME to pick up some gear for tonight's festivities. While I did that I called Arnie but there was no answer. I called Samantha next.

"Hello?" she said.

"Hi, Samantha. Leo."

"How are you?"

"Fine I guess. How about you?"

"Okay. What are you doing?" she asked.

"I'm at home, putting some things together."

"Oh. Do you have any plans for tonight?"

"Yeah. I probably won't be home tonight."

"You're looking for that pimp," she said flatly.

"Yeah. I have to talk to him."

"Talk my ass. I told you, I know that look. I've seen it before. You've got windmills in your eyes, Leo. That spells trouble. Take Arnie with you at least."

"I can't do that."

"Why not? It's his life, his work."

"Maybe, but he's done his bit, remember. He's answered all the calls he ever has to."

She was silent for a while. "You know, right now I fucking hate you. You call up to tell me you're going out to risk your life cleaning up somebody else's mess. It's me they're going to call from the morgue and, thank you very much, I'm not going to wait up for you." She slammed down the phone.

She had a point. Then why was I going out tonight to tangle with this lunatic? Because I wasn't going out there to die. Not me. A failure of imagination? Perhaps that's what heroes and fools share. Right up to the very end. Maybe that's where the difference lies. Heroes exit on their feet, fools go out in a bag. Maybe.

I took the time to update my logs on the case, put my gear in a bag, locked up and left. On the way downtown I swung by Arnie's. He wasn't there. Or he wasn't answering the door. Either way, my card wasn't there.

I stopped at the club for a workout and got all I could handle in an impromptu racquetball match with "Danny C. Rollout," the killshot king. At four-thirty I drove into the city. I was early for my meeting with Anita but I was antsy enough to scratch my skin off. I wanted to get this over with. At five I pulled up to her building and buzzed 3G. She answered right away. "Yes?"

"Anita, this is Leo. I know I'm early. Do you want to grab a bite to eat first?"

Silence. "Okay. Let me get dressed. I'll be right down."

She came over to the car dressed in Bimbo Classic: spike heeled boots and a black body stocking with a fake fur jacket for warmth. I gave her the once over. She smiled. "I have to blend in, right?"

"That you do."

We ate at the Old Ebbitt Grill on Fifteenth Street, where she didn't exactly blend in, but she took the stares in stride. After the meal we began to cruise for my last piece of equipment. The choices improve after dark when the dropping temperatures bring them huddling around heat vents and into crevices out of the wind. I found the one I was looking for in an alleyway off Twelfth and G streets. Curled up on his side, snoring with his mouth open, he lay beneath the exhaust vent of Blenheim's Bakery. I propped him up under the armpits and tried to avoid his breath—a mix of equal parts vomit and red wine. He was the right size. The shoes would be the hard part.

"Partner, can you hear me?"

"Hunh?"

"You want to make some easy money? A C-note, right here and now?"

"Sure. Whatcha wanna do?" He was running his tongue around inside his mouth and over his oddly spaced teeth. At the end of each lap his mouth popped open with a clack.

"I want to buy your clothes. That's all. Then I'm gonna take you out and buy you a nice dinner."

He stopped clacking and a feral wariness crept into his eyes. "You a queer?"

"No. I just want to buy your clothes and I'll make it worth your while."

He started clacking again and his eyes flashed up and down the alley. Anita was sitting in the Camaro. Its sleek shape and dusky color made it blend into the night. The only working streetlight was at the far end of the alley. It threw an angled light over the strange topography: jagged fences, staggered rows of garbage cans, squatting dumpsters, and slick, roll-up loading gates. The shadows added an immensity and depth to the buildings around us, making the alley into a canyon. The old man looked around and saw no one else but me.

He moaned and threw his arms up before him. "Don't kill me, please."

"What?"

He started to slide down the wall until he was curled up at my feet. His hands were laced across the top of his head and his arms and shoulders were hunched up. "Do it quick. Please. I can't run no more." A tremor ran through his legs like a death spasm.

I reached down and pulled the old man up by the arm. "I'm not going to hurt you. I just want your clothes. I'm willing to pay for them." He avoided my eyes — the animal sign of submission. I guess it did seem pretty crazy to want to buy his clothes. I gave it one last try. "I'll pay you one hundred dollars and then I'll take you to any restaurant you want for a nice hot meal. What do you say? My car's right here."

Hunger, greed, curiosity, something subdued his fear and he walked down the alley towards my car.

Anita looked at me. "What's this?"

"A prop. Let him in the back."

She rolled down her window and rolled up her eyes when he slid past her. As he settled into the car he gave one last look at his home. A trace of fear was still in his eyes, the lingering doubt that instead of a hot meal there was just a pine box at the end of this trip. I drove slowly up the alley. Anita eyed me warily. The old man kept clacking his tongue. We nosed out of the alley and slipped into traffic. I wanted the old man out of this section of town.

"What do you like to eat?"

"Anything. Mostly soft stuff. My teeth ain't so good any more. I don't like soup much, though."

"How about Chinese food, dumplings?"

"Yeah, I like that Chinese food." He clacked.

"Dim sum it is then. All you can eat."

I turned right on H Street and drove into Chinatown. There was a carryout between Sixth and Seventh that made great dim sum. I pulled up to the curb and gave Anita a twenty. "Get a big assortment. A beer for him, a glass of water for me, and whatever you want to drink."

"Whatever you say, boss." She took the twenty carefully, trying not to touch my hand. Perhaps she thought that my mental disorder was contagious.

She brought back a foil-wrapped platter, two beers and a large cup of water. I pulled into a nearby parking lot and we ate. The old guy must have been starving. When he finished the platter, I asked Anita to go back for another and a second round on the drinks.

When she returned, she handed the stuff in through the window. The old man grabbed the platter, tore off the foil and popped a pastry into his mouth. With each chew his face seemed to fold in on itself like an accordion. His nose almost touched his chin. Then miraculously it reinflated itself with all his features in the right place.

Anita climbed in, leaned back against the door and handed me the cup of water. "Have you got a kidney infection or something?"

"Nope, just getting ready for the night."

"What?"

"Don't worry about it. It's my problem."

"I can see that."

The old guy finished off most of the platter. Anita and I nibbled a few pieces off it. He wiped his mouth with his sleeve, ignoring a pile of napkins that came with the tray.

"God, that was good."

I finished my glass of water and hooked an arm over the car seat. "Okay ace, time to conclude our business." Reaching into my wallet I took out a C-note, folded it lengthwise and held it out to him. "Now we trade clothes."

"Whatever you say."

I drove in a loop through Chinatown and found another alley two blocks over. I pulled all the way into it where it crossed the *T* with another alley. In the darkness I killed the engine and the lights, climbed out with my bag in hand and motioned for the old man to get out. I looked in at Anita. "I'll be back in a minute."

"Don't be in such a hurry. This car smells like a sewer. Give me a break, huh?"

"Sure thing." I gave her the keys. "If anyone comes up here, turn on your lights and drive away real casually. Go around the block and pick me up where the other alley comes out."

I led the old man up the alley to the darkest spot and told him to take off his clothes. I did the same until we were both in our underpants and socks. Then we exchanged jackets, shirts, pants and shoes. I took his hat.

When he was done dressing he looked down at himself, "That's it, huh?" He couldn't quite believe it.

"Yeah, that's it. Just like I said. Now get." He slid past me, still eyeing me warily for that last-second shiv in the ribs. Once by me he scrambled up the alley to the street and was gone.

I cinched the pants tight with his rope belt. His shoes fit, but more importantly the soles were good so I could kick with them. I unzipped my bag and began to rummage through it.

"Nice body."

Startled, I looked up. Anita was standing there, hands on hips, staring at me.

"You look bigger without your clothes on." She continued to appraise me as I got dressed. "Do you work out a lot?"

"When I can, but I'm not a bodybuilder or anything."

"Don't apologize. I don't like a man who's more into his body than mine."

I let that pass. "Why aren't you in the car?"

"I wanted to see what you were doing."

"Well, now you know. I'm going to be giving you some instructions to follow later on and you had better do as I say. If you don't we could both wind up dead. Do you understand?"

"I understand. Do you think you can take Jack?"

"I wouldn't be here if I didn't, now would I?"

"Well excuse me." Anita walked briskly back to the car. Her stride was long and fluid, capped with a crisp carriage return of the hips.

I slipped leather gauntlets on my forearms and decided against the Kevlar vest. The Arkansas Toothpick is a stabbing knife not a slashing one and it'll go through Kevlar like butter even if a .357 won't. If Jack fancied himself the man of steel he'd use it that way. I took out a jar of grease and soot and daubed my face with the streaks of a man who carelessly wipes or picks at his face with a filthy sleeve. I rubbed some of the mix on my neck and hands. Next, I slipped on a pair of worn leather sap gloves. There was a half pound of lead sewn in across the knuckles. Then on with the shirt and jacket. Last I plopped his soft hat on my head. I stood there trapped in that old man's stink. I wasn't sure I'd ever get that smell out of my mind. The clothes were stiff with urine, vomit, wine and sweat. I was a standing ruin and a monument to a life gone awry.

After putting my wallet and gun into my bag, I walked back to the car. Anita was behind the wheel, staring at me with a strange mixture of loathing and awe. I climbed into the car. "Do you know where Eldorado Jack hangs out?"

"Yeah, Wanda showed me once."

"Okay. Drop me two blocks north of that on the corner.

That'll be Fourteenth and K. Drive past Jack's corner and then up H Street. Park as close as you can, get out and wait. You're the observer. Keep Jack in sight. Don't look for me. I'll get there. When it's done, go back to the car and wait for me. I'll get to you. Keep my bag on the front seat, unzipped. Got it?"

"Got it. Jesus, do you stink."

"I know. I'm inside, remember."

Chapter 17

FIFTEEN MINUTES LATER I climbed out of the car, slammed the door and looked down Fourteenth Street. A gap in the traffic appeared and I shuffled into the moving crowd. People moved away as I passed among them. I meekly met their eyes, embarrassed at my stench. Perhaps after a while you don't care. Those that looked back at me did so with anger. I was offensive, a blot, disgusting. I swallowed, grinned ashamedly and shuffled along. I crossed the street and on the opposite corner stumbled into a couple hurrying by. The boy—he was no more than that—slammed me in the shoulder. I rocked back.

"Hey, man, the fuck's the matter with you?" he yelled.

I shrugged harmlessly and mumbled, "Sorry."

"Sorry? You sure are a sorry mutha fucka. You stinking up the whole street." People hurried by, eyes down.

"I said I was sorry." I snuck a look at him. His hair was long, slick with some gel and crinkled. A pencil-thin mustache and wispy goatee framed his thick lips.

"Maybe you don't know how bad you smell, old man? Maybe you need your nose cleaned? Huh?"

I wasn't about to let this little shit do me, but I surely didn't want to coldcock him. After all, I was just a harmless bum.

"How about maybe I just cut you fuckin' nose off? Huh?" He was bouncing around on his toes, revving himself up, looking back and forth from me to the woman he was with. She was a veteran of the streets and was looking up and down the sidewalk for The Hoss.

"How about I cut his nose off, mama? What you think?" His hand was moving towards his back pocket. I hoped she was a vegetarian.

"Come on, man, we don't need no trouble." She was yanking on his arm. "You wanted a good time, right, baby? Come on, I show you a good time." She licked her lips. He started off with her. As he walked away he turned back and shook his finger at me. "You lucky, old man. I'd a cut your nose off, mutha fucka, but I'm a lover not a fighter." He chuckled. I hoped his dick fell off.

After another block I had my hangdog shuffle down pat. A little bit of side-to-side wobble, a little bit of limp-leg drag-along. My kidneys hurt. I'd had too much to drink. I reached back to knead one. As a final touch I started to mumble to myself. I droned on, shaking my head as if the words were trapped inside like the last pennies in a piggybank, hoping they'd drop out of my mouth and leave me alone.

I crossed another street and my back was hurting worse. Up ahead on the corner Jack was holding court. His cherry red wagon was pulled up to the curb. Jack sat inside with the door open. The car's T.V. was on. The stereo was blaring. As I wobbled up the street, a number of girls came to the door and spoke to Jack and left. With some he was tender, cooing, cupping their chins in his hand, kissing them lightly. With one girl, he grabbed her wrist, pulled her close to him, said something in her ear and then cracked her across the face one solid stinging blow. Her head snapped back and tears welled up in her eyes. Jack wagged his finger at her. "You hold out on me, sugar, I'll retire you. Blind men won't fuck you. You hear me?"

She nodded.

"I don't hear you, bitch."

"Yes, Daddy Jack, I hear you."

"Good." Jack waved her off and she clattered away on her heels.

Jack slid out of the car and stretched himself. Today he wore sky blue pointy-toed boots and a lemon yellow silk suit over a sky blue silk shirt open halfway to his crotch.

He was going to wish he'd worn red. He shook out his arms and tugged on the French cuffs of his shirt so that the large gold cufflinks he wore could be seen. Jack checked the feel of his collar, ran his hands through his wavy hair and looked up and down the street. Checking the turf.

I went on shuffling and mumbling down the street. Jack's eyes passed over me. There was no change in expression. I was beneath his contempt. Jack leaned against the front quarterpanel of his car. Three of his girls were with him, talking and laughing. They bantered with passing men. People passing by all snuck a look at the man, his women, and his car. The door was open to show off the bar, the T.V., the fur seats and carpet. I looked at Jack one last time. He was smiling as he surveyed all that was his. A man at peace with himself. God my back hurt. I took a deep breath; it was now or never. Look out, Jack, I'm gonna rain on your parade.

Jack was facing away from me, talking to a girl and another pimp. I lurched across the sidewalk towards the car, leaned against its open doorway, unzipped my fly and pissed all over his white fur seats.

"Goddamn, man, what the fuck you doin?" Jack spun me around. I pissed all over his shirt and pants.

"You fuckin' son-of-a-bitch, I'll kill you." Jack, bug-eyed and snarling with rage, was starting to turn purple. He looked down at himself and then into his car with disbelief. I zipped up my fly and took a step back. A still zone of silence had spread around us. Jack whipped the blade out from under his left armpit. I licked my lips. A wave of fear left me nauseated. The blade was easily seven inches long and grew from his palm like a shiny sixth finger. Jack circled me, legs apart, up on the balls of his feet. His eyes were locked on my face. Where the head goes the body must follow. He stabbed upward, right to left. I leaped back. The blade whizzed by my face. His arm looped around and he lunged at my belly. I sidestepped, sucking in my gut like a toreador. Jack passed me and stabbed backwards at my face. The steel burned. I bled from jaw to nose. Jack pirouetted and stalked me. Voices cried, "Stick him, stick him. Make him pay, Jack. Cut him!" Jack stabbed again, right to left. I whipped my head away, spraying blood in a wide arc. The blade skidded off my left gauntlet. The artery was safe. Again the loop and lunge. I spun away and casually cuffed him with the sap glove. He staggered away holding his head. Then he whirled back around.

"What's a matter, Jack, that old man hurt you?" the other pimp cackled.

Final exams were coming up. I wondered how good a student Jack was. Did he know that third on a match is a dead man? Again the same outward stab and loop. Again Jack lunged at my belly. This time, I pivoted inside the lunge, where my work would be invisible, and climbed up his body. Heel to instep, elbow to belly, leaden backhand to his nose. Jack staggered away, gasping for air and spouting blood from his mashed nose. Splotches of blood flecked his jacket and shirt. I slowly circled him. Still dragging my leg, I began to mumble to myself. Went to the well once too often, Jack. He was doubled over with his back to me. He seemed to be reaching into his coat pocket for something. I tensed. He turned back slowly, still doubled over, both arms pulled into his chest.

Two other pimps appeared and began laughing. Word was spreading. I flicked a quick glance at the crowd. Two of Jack's girls were smiling faintly. Anita looked excited. Mumbling, I closed slightly with Jack. He stared at me. Come and get it, scumbag.

Jack uncoiled and leaped at me. Left hand up, he flung something at my eyes. I flinched and raised my arms. The blade came up under them. A single point of steel flew at my heart. No time to move. Crossed wrist parry. Steel strikes leather. I grabbed his wrist. He pushed on, all his weight behind the blade. I turned sideways, sliding my arms and his thrust away from my body. As the blade passed my chest, I twisted his arm and screwed it into the shoulder socket. Locked in place, my lead fist easily shattered the elbow. I leaned away and casually snap-kicked his right knee. The joint caved in and the ligaments snapped like rubber bands. Jack crumpled and fell amid a chorus of laughter. He lay there moaning on the sidewalk. It sounded like he was trying to sing around a tongue depressor. His right arm and leg looked like they had been put on backwards.

One of the pimps looked down at Jack. "Big Bad Jack had hisself an accident, huh?" Then he spit on him. Heads were shaking. Jack's girls were talking to other pimps. I heard one say, "Sheeit, ain't that somethin', old wino kick his fuckin' ass. Musta been a fighter one time." Anita was gone. The sirens were getting louder. The crowd was leaving the scene. I joined them.

I turned down the side street, keeping to the storefront shadows. Two blocks away I could see the taillights of a car parked at the corner. Just two blocks. My face was on fire. I was afraid to touch it with my filthy fingers, so I poked at it with my tongue. Slowly I moved it across the inside of my mouth. My tongue didn't come through into the cold night. Thank you, God. A rivulet of blood was running down my cheek. It was warm and it pulsed. He hit an artery. I was in deep trouble. I staggered on towards the car. I focused on the taillights and counted them as I plodded on. One. Two. Left. Right. One foot. Two foot. Almost there. A piece of cake. A figure appeared. No place to run to. I took a deep breath. The rivulet ran faster. I was getting woozy. She moved towards me like solid darkness. I was turning into smoke.

Chapter 18

AN ARM SLID AROUND MY WAIST and I toe-walked like an
unstrung puppet up the street. I looked over and saw Anita
staring at me. "Jesus Christ, look at your face." She pulled
open her purse, took out a handkerchief, folded it back and
pressed it against my face. "Hold this against it, hard!"
When we arrived at the car, she slid me into the front seat
and buckled me up. I leaned my head back.

Five minutes later we were pulling into the emergency
entrance of a nearby university hospital. Anita jumped
out and ran inside. She came back with an orderly and
a stretcher. I staggered out of the car and climbed onto the
stretcher.

"Jesus, where'd you find this guy?" he said, turning his
head away.

"That's not your problem. Just fix him up," she snapped.

He wheeled me into the emergency room. Anita followed
hard on his heels. An admissions clerk approached me, took
one look and decided I had no useful information to tell
her. Anita said, "I'll give you whatever information you
need."

The orderly pushed me through the doors into the sur-
gical suite. A doctor and nurse were waiting inside for me.
They both winced when I was presented to them.

"Get some air deodorant over here," the doctor said. The
nurse quickly sprayed the whole area. They both donned
gloves before they touched me.

"All right, let's see what we've got here. Hold still, fellah,
I'm going to remove this bandage."

I looked up at the guy. Short, chunky, with a thick black beard, hook nose and heavy-lidded eyes. He looked like a pirate. His name tag said Wasserman. A pirate named Wasserman? Maybe not.

He took the handkerchief off slowly, then quickly pressed it back into place. "Got a little pumper here. We're going to have to ligate it. Let's get an H and H on him. I want his vitals and start an IV. Get me some four by fours, a mosquito clamp and we'll sew things right up."

"Hold it, guys." the other nurse said as she walked in. "You won't believe it, but that woman outside wants a plastic surgeon called in. Skrepinski's on his way down."

"Christ, are you kidding?" Wasserman wailed. "All right, let's just close the bleeder off."

In the next couple of minutes the nurse stuck me more often than Jack had. I had an IV in my arm, and as if I could spare it, they had taken more blood. Dr. Wasserman returned, slowly removed the gauze pad he'd put on over the slash, irrigated the area and then said, "The next thing I do will hurt a bit. Just look away and—"

"Jesus," I groaned. While he was talking to me the sneaky bastard had clamped off the artery.

He closed it off quickly and taped a gauze pad across my face. "Okay, you won't bleed any more from that. The plastic surgeon will be down shortly." He stripped off his gloves, tossed them into the trash can and pulled the curtain around me.

I lay there trying to evade the throb of my face. I imagined my face as a launch pad, loading my mind into a rocket and then blasting off into space. I never made lift-off. Finally, Dr. Skrepinski arrived.

He looked like a good advertisement for his own work. His unlined face with its perfect features and even tan bespoke a man who appreciated vanity in his own life. He flipped through the chart, reading it aloud to himself. "Facial laceration, mandibular edge to nares of the nose, approximately four inches. Transverse facial artery severed and ligated. No involvement of the parotid duct gland or the masseter. Very good." He turned to look at me, the flesh and blood equivalent of all those fancy phrases.

"So you don't want the Heidelburg U. varsity letter, eh?" Cute. He went on. "How did this happen?"

"I fell."

"Of course. Are you allergic to any medications? Any history of heart or lung diseases? Are you taking any medication?"

"No, no and no."

"Fine."

The nurse reappeared. He looked up and gave her her marching orders. "Set up a sterile plastics set: twenty-six gauge needle, one-half percent Xylocaine, Betadine, six-oh nylon."

"Have you ever had a tetanus shot before?" the nurse asked.

"Yeah, but I don't remember when."

She placed a syringe and a small vial on the doctor's tray. It was all silverware and nothing to eat.

"Okay. Let's make sure you haven't severed any muscles or nerves. Turn your face to the left. Now the right. Open your mouth. Close it. Clench your teeth. Smile. Grimace. Excellent." He washed out my mouth with alcohol and I hadn't even said a bad word yet.

"Okay. I'm going to make some injections into your face, oh, say, about half a dozen. They'll burn for a second like a bee sting, say, then your face will go numb and I'll fix you right up. You'll look as good as new." He stopped for a second and looked surprised that he had wasted that promise on someone like me.

"Okay. Don't move now. Hold on to the stretcher and turn your eyes away."

I gripped the side of the stretcher and tensed up. This was worse than messing with Jack. The needle loomed in the corner of my eye, a steel hummingbird moving towards my face. I was ready to run or scream. I closed my eyes and the bee stung me. Quickly the rest of the hive arrived. My face filled up with ice and its contours softened and disappeared.

"The worst is over. Just relax and we'll sew this right up."

He swabbed my face, covered everything but the slash with sterile towels and went to work. When he finished and took off the towels I looked at the E.R. clock. He'd been working on me for an hour and a half.

"Okay. We're done." He stripped off his gloves. "Come to my office in three days and we'll remove the stitches then. I'll order something for pain if you'd like. Keep the area clean and dry and take a bath before you come to the office." He wasn't smiling.

"Right and thanks."

"You're welcome." With that he was gone.

The nurse came in and undid my IV. She gave me a card with follow-up care instructions and the surgeon's name and address on it. I had to ride in a wheelchair out to the car. Anita pulled up and she and the nurse hoisted me out of the chair and into the car.

At home Anita helped me into a bath, trashed my clothes and scrubbed the places I couldn't reach. Snugly between clean sheets, I slipped effortlessly into sleep. My last sight was of her undressing before the mirror. She was stroking her nipples and smiling.

Chapter 19

I WOKE UP AROUND TEN. My face had been returned to me, complete with throb and burn. I struggled out of bed and went to the bathroom. Brushing my teeth was a terrifying idea. I gargled gingerly instead and went into the kitchen. Anita was sitting in the eating nook, looking out at the street with a cup of coffee cradled in her hands.

"Morning," I said.

"How are you feeling?"

"Better. Clean for starters, which is wonderful. My face hurts but not too bad."

I poured myself a cup of coffee, put a lot of milk in it and hesitantly sipped it. As I sat down, Anita pulled a business card from her purse.

"Here. Wanda said call her at this number." I pulled the phone over to the table and dialed the number.

"Hello."

"Wanda Manlove, please."

"This is Wanda Manlove speaking. Can I help you?"

"Leo Haggerty calling."

"Very good. I like your work very much. I had a friend check out 'our friend's' condition. Broken nose, concussion, shattered knee and elbow. He'll be in a wheelchair for two months. Seems you can't use crutches when your arm and leg are broken on the same side. What a shame. Six months in casts, then six more of rehabilitation. Word is he'll never recover full use of either. He couldn't pimp ice cubes in August around here."

"Okay. I delivered. Now it's your turn."

"Where and when?"

"Your place in an hour?"

"Fine." She hung up.

My face was starting to hurt. I went back to the bathroom and popped a couple of pills. Anita was in the doorway, still with a cup of coffee in her hands.

"Listen, I want to thank you for getting a plastic surgeon. I wouldn't have thought of that and the other E.R. doctor looked like he'd just as soon have sewn me up with a shoelace."

She shrugged. "Why get your face messed up if it isn't necessary. Besides, I can afford it. And now you owe me one. I like the idea of you owing me one. Never can tell when I'll need your help."

"How do you know I'd pay you back?"

"I don't. But I think you will. I consider it another investment. I've done very well with mine so far."

"I'm sure you have. Buy low and sell high."

"That's not nice. Why not get dressed and I'll drive us over to Wanda's?"

"Sure."

Twenty minutes later I was being let into their apartment. Anita started to follow me in when Wanda said, "Anita, I've run out of cigarettes. Would you mind getting me some?" Wanda's look said, Start with raw tobacco. Age it six months.

"Sure, Wanda. Whatever," she said sarcastically.

I sat down with my old friend the wooden drunk, crossed my arms and waited for her to start. Wanda took the throne chair, lit a cigarette and blew a long plume of smoke.

"First things first. Stand up. I want to make sure you aren't wired."

"You must have some story to tell."

"Stand up."

"No problem." I stood up, hands high. Wanda patted me down very well.

"Okay. Sit down. What do you want to know?"

"For starters, were you in the room with Malcolm Donnelly the night he died?"

"Yes."

"How did he contact you?"

"Lobby phone, I guess. I tell clients never to use their room phones."

"Did you know him before?"

"Yeah. He was a regular. We'd gotten together a few times. Mostly, he was a contractor. He hired me out to entertain clients."

"What kind of clients?"

"Government types, military guys. Malcolm was a contracting officer with some consulting firm. They had lots of government contracts. I was a little 'gift' he used to close a deal. Hell, he even wrote me off as a deductible expense on his contracting costs. Anyway, he called me up, asked me to come over and bring some gin with me. He wanted the usual—an overnight.'

"The usual?"

"Yeah. After he'd nail down a contract, he'd want to celebrate. So he'd tell his wife he had to travel. Someplace not too far away so he didn't need a lot of documentation. We'd get a hotel room, spend the night and celebrate. Things must have been tough on Malcolm these days. I hadn't heard from him in quite a while."

"Did he write that off too?"

"Knowing Malcolm, I'm sure he did."

"What do you go for, by the way?"

"Don't ask. You can't afford me."

"Humor me."

"Five hundred a night." She stubbed out her cigarette.

"Okay. So he called you up. Then what?"

"So I picked up the booze and went over to see him. I presumed he had something to celebrate. I went through the lobby, took an elevator up, knocked and he let me in."

She lit up another cigarette and crossed her lovely legs.

"Then what?" I crossed mine.

"He looked like hell when I got there. I mean like he was sick or something. It must have come on him real quick because he sounded fine on the phone. I began to worry. Let me tell you, business is off all around. This AIDS shit has done more for chastity than all the sermons in history. I was afraid he was sick like that. I was ready to bolt."

"What did he look like?"

"He was flushed, you know, and sweating. His hands were shaking. He said he felt hot and he loosened his tie. I sat down and asked him if he wanted a drink. He said no. Anyway, he was pacing all around and looked real tense, uptight, you know. He didn't look like he was up for anything. So I told him we'd do it another time, but he said no, he'd be okay. Then he sits down and makes a phone call."

"What'd he say, exactly?"

"All right, let me think." She put her hands to the sides of her head and closed her eyes. "He said, 'Doc, this is Malcolm. I feel like hell. This is worse than ever.' Something like that, yeah. Then whoever was on the phone said something and he said, 'Are you sure it's okay?' Then the other person said something, and then Malcolm gave him the address and the room number." She pulled out another cigarette. "He asked me for the gin. I took the bottle out and gave it to him. He poured himself a drink and downed it. Then I saw him take out a bottle of pills. Anyway, I went into the bathroom to change. He was a garter belt freak. When I came out, he was out in the chair. So I figured, fuck it, this is a waste. I got dressed and split. That's it."

"Why'd you ask around about him?"

"I just wanted to be sure he hadn't gotten it into his head to talk to security about me."

"Why would he do that?"

"Some johns get pissed if you leave them. It's like you're supposed to stay around at their beck and call, no matter what shape they're in. I didn't want him to finger me to security, if he was pissed. I do a lot of business out of there."

I uncrossed my legs, stood up, looked down at her and began to clap. "Bravo. An excellent performance. You're a hell of an actress, but then that's the heart of the work, isn't it?"

"What do you mean? I told you the truth!" She recrossed her arms and legs in a huff.

"Like hell you did. Actually, you probably were telling the truth right up to the end there. That last part was right out of the *Twilight Zone*."

"I don't have to take this shit."

"Oh yes you do, darling." I walked around and then turned back to her. "What time did you go into his room?"

"A little after five, I guess."

"And you left when?"

"I don't know. A half hour later. No more."

"Isn't that interesting. Right around the time of death. I'll tell you what I'm going to do. I'm going to give you one more chance to get your story straight. Then I call the police, and give you to them. Maybe they can pin his death on you. Even if they can't, your low-profile lifestyle is over. I've got some friends at the paper. Maybe we can make you page one, with photos."

"You double-crossing son-of-a-bitch."

"Not hardly. You're lying to me. I know you are. You wouldn't respect me if I let you get away with that."

"Fuck you."

"You cost too much, remember." I went to the phone and picked it up.

"All right, damn you. That's not what happened."

I put down the phone. "What did happen?"

"When I come out he was in the chair. He wasn't out though. He was dead."

"Did you go over to look at him?"

"Yes, I did."

"Then what?"

"Then I split like I said."

"You sent Francine around to see if you'd been tagged coming in or going out?"

"Right."

"But not because of Donnelly talking to anyone."

"No. I was worried about a murder rap. I just freaked

out. I wasn't thinking clearly. I kept thinking about that woman and Belushi. I did give him the drink. Anyway, I sent Francine down the next day. After she told me no one saw me, I calmed down and thought about it some more. There was no way they could tag me with murder, but an investigation like that would be hell on business. I just wanted to keep out of it. I mean, it's too bad the guy died and all, but it wasn't my fault. Why not just walk away from it, right?"

"But you didn't just walk away from it, did you?"

"What do you mean?"

"What I mean is that you were so shook up about seeing that dead man, that you freaked out, right?"

"Yeah, it was awful."

"I'm sure it was. It must have been a nail-shattering experience. So you got dressed and split right away. Only first you took the five hundred dollars from his wallet. Not too freaked out to rob a dead man, were you?"

Her eyes burned into mine. "So what if I did? You can't prove it. That money was owed me. It isn't my fault he died before I could earn it. Anyway, he was just a john. He didn't give a shit about me. Why should I be broken up about him?"

"I haven't the slightest idea why. But even war has its rules, Wanda. One of them is that you shoot looters on sight. Even your own side's." I made a gun out of my hand and pointed it at her. She gave me the finger as I walked out.

In the hall, as I waited for the elevator, I tried to figure out a reason for Wanda to bring a typed suicide note with her for her liaison with Donnelly and came up short. It just didn't fit with the rest of her story. There was no reason for her to take the pills and leave the gin she'd bought. No, Wanda didn't make the big board. According to Wanda, Marta Vasquez couldn't have killed her husband. So she had no reason to plant a suicide note after the fact. It was time for Marta Vasquez's name to come down. However, someone named Doc had just gone to the head of the class.

Anita stepped out of the elevator and stopped right in front of me.

"Your business with Wanda done?"

"Yeah, I think so."

"Good. By the way, I met your girlfriend this morning." I didn't like the wicked gleam in her eyes. "Jesus Christ. What did you tell her?" I almost didn't want to know.

"I told her you were in bed. You'd had a rough night and I'd brought you home and tucked you in."

"Great. Thanks a lot. Shit." My mind was whirling uselessly, like a disengaged gear, as I tried to calculate how much damage she'd done.

"It was the truth."

"But not the whole truth. If you've fucked this up for me—"

"Shh." She put her finger against my lips. "Don't make idle threats. Besides, you owe me one. And I like you. A lot. I can be a lot of fun."

"Why don't I believe that?" I said as I hurriedly backed away from her into the elevator.

Chapter 20

I CALLED SAMANTHA immediately and got her machine. I left a long message anyway asking her to call me on my car phone at any time. Then I called Marta Vasquez and asked her if she knew of any friends of her husband's who were nicknamed Doc. She said she'd never heard him call anyone that. I asked her to get together his address book, all his credit card statements, check stubs and health insurance claims for the last year. I told her I'd be over to get the information from her.

In the car I took a second to lie back and close my eyes. The incision throbbed and my face felt like someone was tunneling a transatlantic cable through it. I tried a smile on for size and it hurt worse. Driving over to Marta Vasquez's I prayed that my phone would ring. It didn't. I trudged grimly up to the front door. Just as I was about to knock on the door, Marta Vasquez pulled it open. "Please come in, Mr. Haggerty."

"Thanks. Can I have a glass of water, please?"

"Surely." She walked back towards the kitchen. Over her shoulder she asked, "What happened to your face?"

"I cut it shaving."

"You must be very clumsy."

"Touché."

She returned and held out a glass of water. I took it, said thanks, popped a painkiller in my mouth and drowned it.

Marta wore a burgundy sweater tucked into blue jeans. The jeans were tucked into high, cordovan boots. Her hair was pulled straight back and highlighted her black eyes and lush mouth. Whatever Malcolm Donnelly couldn't find at home it wasn't sexual.

"Do you have the information I asked for?"

"Yes. It's on the dining room table."

"Great."

"Do you want anything to eat?"

"No, thanks. I'm drinking my meals these days."

"Some soup, then. I have some homemade *sopa de ajo*. It's very good for shaving cuts." She smiled.

"Thanks."

I went to the table. On it were a pad and pencil, a checkbook, a manila folder and an address book. I sat down, opened the checkbook and made a list of all the checks made out to physicians. Then I went through the folder that contained his credit card receipts and added any new names to the first list. A review of the year's medical claims did not yield any additional names. Then I went through the address book and wrote down the phone numbers and addresses for the names on the list. There were seven names. Six physicians and a pharmacy.

"Soup's on."

I took my list and went into the kitchen. A large bowl of soup with a thick slice of a dense, dark bread next to it was set out for me. I sat down and Marta pulled up a chair catty-corner to mine with soup and bread of her own.

The soup was hot and spicy, redolent with garlic. I tore off chunks of the bread and dunked them in the soup. Properly softened, I was able to get them down. I slid the list over to Marta. "What can you tell me about these names?"

I sipped my soup as she scanned the list.

"Dr. Carson was our dentist."

"For all of you?"

"Yes."

"Dr. Canzoneri was Malcolm's physician. He's an internist. I went to him also. Dr. Harrison is my OB-GYN. Dr. Locke is my eye doctor; I wear contacts. Dr. Reece is the kids' pediatrician. Dr. Tompkins is Cholo's vet. Cholo is our boxer." I looked around for said animal. "He's at Dr. Tompkins's right now. His ears were just cropped and I think he's got an infection in one of them." She handed me the list and I scribbled some notes on it.

"Would you hand me the phone, please? I'm going to call these people." She reached over, grabbed the phone, freed up some cord and handed it to me. "And thanks for the soup. It was just right."

"*Por nada.*"

Harrison, Locke and Reece had never seen Malcolm Donnelly as a patient. Carson was a solo practitioner and had been out of town on the day Malcolm Donnelly died. Donnelly's call from the hotel had been local. Four down, one to go. Dr. Canzoneri's office refused to give me any information. When Mr. Donnelly paid the overdue balance on his bill they would be glad to speak with me. Until then Consolidated Collection Corporation spoke for them. I drew question marks after Canzoneri's name. It would be interesting to know whether he had treated Malcolm for gonorrhea, and when. That left the pharmacy.

Marta asked, "Would you like some coffee?"

"Thanks, plenty of milk with it, though."

"Sure." She stood up and went to the sink.

With her back to me she asked, "Why are you so interested in Malcolm's doctors?"

"I want to know where he got the medicine that was in his system when he died. I think he might have had a prescription for it after all."

"What is it called?"

"Meprobamate. I don't know what the brand name would be."

"Let me look in the medicine chest. See if we have it there. I don't remember it, though. Malcolm hated drugs. You could hardly get him to take aspirin for a headache." She washed her hands and walked out of the kitchen.

She came back with three jars and a bottle. They contained a common antihistamine, a painkiller, an antidiarrhea medicine and a cough medicine with codeine. All of which were over two years old.

"This is all we have. I knew I hadn't seen any new pills recently. Why do you think he had a prescription for it?"

Truth and consequences time. "Your husband was not alone on the night he died. A high-priced call girl was with him. She says that he looked sick and that he had some pills with him. I'm trying to find out where he got them from."

"Was she with him when he died?"

"Yes."

She looked at me expectantly.

"She said that he looked sick, but he didn't want to die. He wanted to live. He called a doctor for help. She went into the bathroom and when she came back out he was dead. It must have been very sudden. He didn't cry out or anything."

"Do you believe her?"

"Yes."

"Will she say this in court?"

"If she's approached properly, I think she will." Like with a two by four.

"How does this change things?"

"It opens up the possibility of malpractice. I'm certain that Malcolm didn't commit suicide. Now it's a question of whether he died by accident or from negligence. Either of those findings is more consistent with his behavior that day. If Malcolm spoke to a doctor and did something on that doctor's advice and died from it, that makes the doctor responsible."

She didn't bring up and I decided not to remind her about that very bothersome suicide note. Marta went back to making the coffee. After she had it going she turned around and wiped her hands on a towel. "I'm glad he didn't suffer." She went on wiping her hands. "Maybe it's better that he didn't want to die. I don't know. At least I can tell the children that their father didn't want to leave them and know that it's the truth."

"It'll spare them a lot of guilt on top of everything else. Now if I can just prove what I've told you."

The coffee was done. Marta poured two cups and brought

them to the table with cream and sugar. I kept doodling around the pharmacy's name.

"I have an idea. I want you to make a phone call."

"Okay, who do you want me to call?"

"The pharmacy. Tell them that your husband has died. Tell them that for estate purposes — taxes and insurance and so on — you'd like a complete list of his prescriptions including the doctor's name and the date of each prescription."

"Okay."

I passed the phone and the pad to her. Five minutes later she hung up the phone and pushed the pad back to me. There was one prescription. It had been refilled three times. Meprobamotrin. Prescribed by a Dr. Truman Whitney, office phone 555-7241.

I picked up the phone and dialed his number. On the fourth ring someone answered and said, "Mental Health Center." I hung up.

"Who was it?"

"A mental health center."

"What?"

"I think your husband was in therapy there. At least, he was going there to get medication."

"But I had no idea. He never told me."

"There were a lot of things he never told you, right?"

"Yes, but there were no records."

"You said your husband was concerned about his security clearance. Therapy is not something you want the clearance investigators to know about. My guess is that he paid for his sessions in cash and never filed for insurance reimbursement."

"What can you do to find out if all this is true?"

"I'm going to pay them a visit and take a look at your husband's chart."

"Will you tell me what you find out?"

"You mean about what Malcolm was doing in therapy?" She nodded. "Are you sure you want to know?"

She sipped her coffee, then put her cup down. "Maybe not. What difference would it make anyway?"

"Probably none." I stood up to leave. Marta followed me to the front door. "Thank you for believing me, Mr. Haggerty."

"Nothing to it. You were telling the truth. I'll be in touch."

I drove home in silence. A cold lump was beginning to form in my chest. Cancer of the heart.

Chapter 21

WHEN I ARRIVED HOME, I raced inside to check my answering service for messages. They had only one message for me. Randi Benson had called.

I rang her at school. "North Hall," a girl's voice said. "Miranda Benson, please. Room 311."

"Hang on I'll get her." Five minutes went by.

"Hello, Leo?"

"Yeah, Randi. How are you?"

"Okay I guess. I need to talk to you."

"What about?"

"I really can't talk about it over the phone. Could you come out and see me?"

"Sure. When?"

"How about tomorrow? I have a lunch break at one."

"Okay. Is this about your father?"

"Isn't it always?"

"All right. See you tomorrow."

Miranda represented my one foray into the role of social worker. It hadn't turned out quite as I had planned. Her therapist had been required by law to report Miranda's sexual abuse by her father. The protective service investigators wanted to take the case to the police and press for criminal charges. After a long conference with my attorney and Benson's attorney, a complicated consent order was entered in juvenile court. A finding of abuse was made and entered in a sealed case file to be stored in Richmond under Miranda's name, not her father's. The record could not be reopened by anyone. Benson agreed to pay for Miranda's boarding school and therapy. In exchange for the return of some photographs, I was made Miranda's legal guardian. I wondered what the bastard was up to now. My face had begun to throb again. Since I had to drive I passed on taking another pill for it. The throb reminded me, however, to call Skrepinski's office. I made an appointment for nine A.M. two days later.

I got dressed to go back into town and check up on Dr. Truman Whitney. Since Malcolm Donnelly had died, his records would not have the usual safeguards of confidentiality. The proper way to do it would be to have Marta, as executor and next of kin, request the records. The center's C.Y.A. committee would convene an in-house proctoscopy and then release the records. Except for that unnecessary suicide note I'd have been glad to do it that way. Whoever left that note in Malcolm's room wouldn't be above purging the records. Time for Dr. Haggerty to make a house call.

I gathered up what I needed, straightened my tie, slipped into my coat and got ready to leave. I left Samantha a message on her machine that I'd be by her place this evening. Going against traffic I had no problem getting back into the city before five P.M. Five o'clock is the magic time, the window of opportunity, for this kind of operation.

At precisely five o'clock I walked up the steps to the mental health center, went around to the entrance marked Emergency Admissions and tried to look like I owned the place. A young black woman with a wiry nimbus of hair and large golden hoop earrings was hustling by with an armful of charts towards a door marked Records Room. I allowed her a decent interval and then followed her in. She was sorting through piles of charts and muttering under her breath. I stood in front of her trying for a look of professional arrogance with a dollop of little boy charm. I wanted her to do what I asked and love doing it.

She looked up at me. "Yes?"

"Hello." I stuck out my hand. She shook it cautiously. "I'm Doctor Yost. I need the records on a patient named Malcolm Donnelly. That's D-O-N-N-E-L-L-Y."

"Sure. Just give me a minute okay? These charts are a mess. What do they think I am, the maid?" She looked back at me. "I haven't seen you here before."

"No. This is my first night on duty. Truman helped me get the job." I hoped Truman was in Ghana for the evening.

"Truman Whitney?"

"Yeah."

"He's all right. You know, I wish they'd tell us when you new guys are gonna start. But then they never tell us night people nothing anyway." She walked over to the floor-to-ceiling files and returned with a manila folder. She extracted a sheet from it and said, "You have to sign for it and put today's date next to your name. When you're done please return all your charts here. Don't make me go around looking for them, okay?"

"No problem. Thanks." I printed Yost and dated it. A quick scan showed that other than Dr. Whitney, only a Dr. Gutierrez had taken out the chart. I memorized the dates on which the chart had been taken out and by whom. She took the sheet back and stuck it in the slot where the record had been.

You don't have to worry about hackers getting into the computers that store confidential information. The leaks created by human hiring policies are enough to do you in. Once social program funds were cut, public mental health center staffs were frozen. All new personnel came on as part-timers or temporaries, and they were usually given the night shift jobs. This kept the centers open around the clock for emergencies. Thus they qualified as a full service center and stayed eligible for whatever funding scraps were left to be had. The turnover rates are terrific. Only vampires work midnight to eight regularly. So you have an endless revolving door of part-time clerical help and rotating emergency service residents hired by people who never see nor talk to them. To get hold of anybody's chart, all you have to do is get on the merry-go-round, claim to be new on the job and look like you belong. I know all this because I once worked undercover in a similar center trying to track down a blackmail ring.

I took the chart to an empty therapist's office. Inside, I closed and locked the door, drew the curtains, flipped on the desk lamp, and sat down to read the record. First, I wrote down the dates it had been taken out and by whom. Then I skimmed the telephone contact sheet, patient information, treatment contract, and consent to exchange information forms. The only useful information was that there were two samples of Malcolm Donnelly's signature. I noted that he'd retained Percy Carleton as his attorney. Percy *vs.* Nate should have been on HBO from Las Vegas. It would have been a hell of a fight. The next page was a medication log. It listed the drug name and dosage, prescription dates, number of pills to be dispensed and instructions for taking them. I wrote down the information about the last prescription: Meprobamotrin, six hundred milligrams, 11/2/86, forty pills, four times a day. A ten-day prescription. There was a closing note on the log: "Informed patient of all risks attached to use of medication, including abrupt termination and extrapyramidal effects with alcohol. Concern over previous Hx of alcohol abuse, r/o alcohol abuse, DSMIII 305.0. Keep dosages sub-lethal. If agitation persists dispense at center to r/o hoarding."

The next pages were actual session notes. My ordinary qualms over reading this stuff had been buried with Donnelly. The first note was an intake:

10/2/86 Presenting problem: Depression. Pt. says it's deepening. Bitter custody battle. Precipitant of crisis: Gonorrhea in wife. She claims he gave it to her. He denies this. Alleges she got it from one of her lovers. She denies any infidelity. Provoked, he hit her. Told her to leave house. She has refused. Very volatile situation. Rec. he consider moving out to cool off situation. Says attorney wants him to stay. Put pressure on wife to leave. Use abandonment as grounds for divorce. Goal: Help control depression and agitation through crisis of impending divorce and custody battle. Informed pt. of limits on confidentiality in court.

10/9/86 Marital Hx: Marriage on rocky ground from start. Met in Argentina. Woman got pregnant. He claims she deceived him about birth control. Married her to do the "right thing." Figured they'd work out their problems later. Stresses brought on by recent failure to be promoted. Felt he needed more money to provide for wife's "unbridled spending." Says he loves wife. Very beautiful. Always wanted the best of everything. He wanted to give it to her. Anxiety and agitation responding to medication. Mood has not lifted.

10/16/86 Pt. wants to cut back frequency of sessions. Not interested in exploring his input into marital situation. Feels problems are all wife's. Clear he wants divorce and custody. Sees sessions as being for symptom relief of anxiety. Doesn't feel like he's "out of control." R/O underlying character pathology.

10/23/86 Pt. very angry. Wife has served him with papers. Refuses to consider mediation or joint custody. Calls wife slut and tramp. Intends to prove she's unfit mother. Says she's taken his money, his love, his self-respect, but "she won't get my kids." Asked if I would testify about his fitness as a parent. Told him such evaluations are a specialty area. Sugg. he consult a forensic psychiatrist or psychologist. Feels she'd just lie and make a good show of it. "Always has been a liar." Can look like great wife and mother when she has to. Wants to hire p.i. to spy on her, catch her with lovers in house, use photos to force her to give up kids.

10/30/86 Abandoned p.i. idea. Cost exorbitant for round-the-clock surveillance. Mood markedly lifted however. Medication finally taking effect? Says he's found solution to his problems. Does abrupt mood shift indicate decision has been made re: suicidal ideation? Pt. resolutely denies any suicidal thoughts. Wants to terminate. Feels it won't look good for a custody case. Manic defense against depression or decompensation? Says he has found expert who will testify to fitness as a parent.

11/6/86 Appt. cancelled. No message. Need to follow-up with T.C.

That was the last entry. Each note had been signed by Dr. Whitney. I closed the case folder and began to scribble notes and questions to myself. That done, I turned off the light, wiped my fingerprints off everything I'd touched and went back to the records room. The night security guard was seated at the front desk, watching the entrance and the waiting room. I walked up to him.

"Excuse me, I'm Dr. Yost. I'm covering for Dr. Whitney this week. Did Mr. Donnelly come in for his appointment last Friday?"

The guard turned to his daily log book and flipped the pages backwards. Over his shoulder I read the entries under Whitney's name. The last entry was a 4:30 walk-in named Poindexter, Cleotus. I scanned the staffing for that night. Gutierrez was not on duty.

"Could he have called in sick or cancelled? He was due in and he shouldn't go this long without his blood levels being checked."

The guard, a bearded black man in his early twenties, twisted back to turn down the sound on the small T.V. on the desk. Captain Kirk was boldly going where no man had gone before. From the look of things there had been good reason to avoid the place. The guard pulled out the phone log and went down the list of that night's calls with his finger. No calls from Donnelly to anyone. "Okay. Thanks. I'd better call the family myself."

Back in the records room, I signed in the Donnelly file and took out the Poindexter case. Since I wasn't going to leave the records room, I didn't have to sign for the chart. Cleotus Poindexter was an ambulatory schizophrenic who heard and often followed a variety of voices. On the date in question, one of them suggested a visit to the nearest mental health center. Cleotus had seen the movie *The Fantastic Voyage* on T.V. and was concerned that a microscopic submarine and crew had been implanted in his penis by his mother and that they were obstructing things and keeping him from getting an erection. Cleotus wanted a catheter inserted and the sub flushed out of there.

Cleotus sounded like one of the casualties of the trend in the '70s to close the mental hospitals and instead let these people wander the streets on thirty-day chemical leashes. Cleotus had his full civil rights to protect him from wrongful imprisonment and damn little to protect him from himself. The important fact was that the billing notation was one and one half hours to Medicare at sixty dollars per hour. Truman Whitney had been occupied with Cleotus Poindexter's delusions when Malcolm Donnelly had died. I was handing the chart back when a yell came from the waiting room area. The records room clerk started up from her desk. I motioned her to sit and said, "I'll look into it." As I started back down the corridor I wondered what the hell I was doing. I was a private investigator, not a psychotherapist. I'd be about as much use up there as a one-legged man at an ass-kicking.

The waiting room was still empty. The guard was on his feet adjusting the television set and muttering, "Holy shit. Holy shit." I came up next to him. The scene was horrifyingly familiar. A lone person, this time a woman. Her face was smudged with something black and she was visibly shaking. She clutched the microphone as if it would turn into a snake. Behind her it was all smoke, screams and sirens. "This is the scene here after the bombs were detonated less than twenty minutes ago. From what we can piece together from talking to survivors, the first bomb was in a bag carried by a young man who placed it on the ground at the intersection of the two wings of the mall. It seems to have been a fragmentation type. Thousands of pieces of metal exploded and flew across this area cutting everyone in their path to ribbons. You can see that all the storefronts in this area have been blown out. The carnage is incredible. There are bodies everywhere. The blood is so thick on the floor it's like syrup. Some of the bodies were . . ." At this she stopped and turned sideways to wipe at her face with her sleeve. "Excuse me. I've never seen anything like this. Some of the bodies were decapitated and many have lost limbs. The second bomb went off approximately one minute later. It caught most of the people who were trying to help the survivors at point blank range. This is Rona Marcus, channel three in Westchester County. We'll have more on our regularly scheduled news at six."

"Jesus fucking Christ. They ought to kill those goddamn bastards," the guard snarled.

"Amen, brother."

A car had pulled up into the parking lot. It was time for me to disappear. I went back to the therapists' offices, followed the exit signs painted on the walls and let myself out a side exit. Like a good boy, I looked both ways before I crossed the street. I walked quickly up the quiet, tree-lined streets of Georgetown. Standing on Wisconsin Avenue, trying not to feel like a target, I couldn't help but think that John Donne's message had finally arrived. From this day forth the bells would toll all over this land.

Chapter 22

MY CAR PHONE RANG while I sat in traffic, growing ever more claustrophobic.

"Hello."

"Leo, I'm returning your message." Samantha said flatly. "I think we should talk, don't you?"

"Absolutely."

"Where are you now?"

"I'm here at the Skyline Dalton. The signing should be over in about an hour."

"Why don't I come down and meet you there?"

"Okay." She hung up.

It took just about the entire hour to get from Georgetown to Bailey's Crossroads. I took the health club elevator down to the shopping mall. A large publicity photo of Samantha was in the bookstore window. Beneath that was a copy of the laudatory reviews that had appeared in the local newspapers. I stood off to the side and watched Samantha signing books and talking to her fans. A woman stood in front of her, her arms clasped around the book like it was a life preserver, and went on about how much she enjoyed Samantha's books and how they spoke to everyone, not just women. The line of true believers wound around the front of the store. I caught the note of contempt in my thoughts, the desire to cut her down to size, and wondered what put it there. Samantha looked like she'd be busy for a good twenty more minutes so I walked over to the bar in a nearby restaurant, pulled up a stool and ordered a drink.

The bar television flashed the presidential seal and then the words Presidential Newscast. The bartender slid my drink over to me, looked at the screen and said, "Want to bet he appoints a committee? The guy passes the buck around like it's a social disease."

"I don't know. He's in a tough spot. He has to try to balance our freedom with the need to protect people. That's a tightrope that gets harder to stay on the slicker it gets with blood. I guess we'll find out what kind of wire-walker lives in the White House."

The local channel logo appeared and then the great one himself filled the screen.

"This evening, my fellow Americans, I want to address the recent terrorist attacks in our great country. They are a threat to all we hold dear, to what makes us the greatest nation on earth, the home of the free and the land of the brave. First, let there be no mistake, the United States will never negotiate with terrorists. Nor will we capitulate to their demands. No dialogue can be forced this way. No grievance can be legitimate that is brought to us soaked in the blood of our citizens. We will interpret all such actions as acts of war against the people of the United States. Any demonstrated connection or support by a foreign power for these acts will draw an immediate reply from the United States. The entire spectrum of response and retaliation will be considered."

"Okay, here comes the committee," the bartender said.

"Give him a chance."

"If we are to survive this attack, if we are to remain the home of the free, we must, more than ever, be the land of the brave. If America is to endure we must have the faith, trust and support of each and every citizen. I have this day authorized funding and staffing for a National Taskforce to Combat Terrorism. This taskforce will coordinate local action plans and make recommendations to congress on national policy. Effective immediately, we are increasing border security and immigration staff to detect, isolate and remove illegal aliens from this country. Victims of terrorist attacks will now be eligible for disaster relief funds. Local officials will now explain what action plans have been implemented in your area. Have patience and courage, and God bless America." With a wave he was gone.

Lieutenant Calvin Simmons appeared on the screen with the unenviable task of translating those grand words into action. He came to the podium, raised his hands to the audience and began to speak.

"Please, I will take questions after I have made my announcement. Please be patient. Credit for the attacks in New York and Los Angeles is now being claimed by a group calling itself The Hand of Allah. They have made no demands at this time. As of now, there seems to be no connection between them and The Standing Committee on World Justice which has claimed credit for the bomb at the Vietnam Veterans Memorial. We have been able to assemble a composite portrait of the man who planted the bomb at the wall from pictures taken by visitors that day. *The Washington Post* and all other local newspapers will carry this picture in tomorrow's editions. The strategy of the attackers, whoever they may be, seems to be to cause maximum death and destruction. They have so far chosen crowded public areas to attack. All federal employees are now on flexi-time schedules to ease rush hour congestion. Some local national guard units will be placed on temporary emergency status to assist in providing security in the downtown areas. We are asking all private businesses to cooperate by putting their employees on flexi-time schedules and to increase security in shopping areas and office buildings. In addition this week's Redskins game against the Raiders has been rescheduled to four o'clock. The gates will open at ten A.M. to begin letting fans in. Expect lengthy delays because of the new security precautions at the stadium. State police will be increasing their patrols of the highways and all abandoned cars will be towed immediately. Above all, each and every citizen should keep his eyes open and report any suspicious activities to a policeman or national guardsman. A toll-free number will be manned around the clock to handle all reports. The number will be 800-FREEDOM."

"What do you think?" the barman asked.

"As a start it's not too bad. I'm not optimistic, though. Pretty soon we'll be seeing militia on the street corners, roadblocks, bomb-sniffing dogs in the schools, bag checks in hospitals, random ID checks. Maybe that'll all look normal to our kids. They won't know that it was ever any different, that there was a time you could walk the streets of America unafraid. They won't know what a precious thing we've lost."

"That's a pretty bleak picture."

"Don't I know it. We've been fat, happy and safe for a long time. I wonder how many payments of this 'tax in blood' we'll have to make before we get smart and ruthless. I guess we'll get as good as or better than anyone else at this once we take it seriously."

I finished my drink, paid the bartender and walked back to the bookstore.

Samantha was standing in the doorway of the store looking up and down the mall for me.

"Hi," I said. "How'd it go?"

"Fine, just fine." Her face was a mask.

"Where do you want to go to talk?"

"My place. That way I can throw you out if I want," she said without the slightest trace of a smile.

"So be it. Did you drive over?"

"No. Sandra dropped me off."

We walked back to my car in silence. I let her in, walked around the car and let myself in. Backing out I broke the silence. "Do you want to hear my side of it?"

"No. I just want you to sit there while I dump all over you. Of course I want to hear your side of it. I'm here to talk and to listen."

"The woman is part of the case, nothing else. She brought me home from the hospital and put me to bed. That's it, period. The end. Nothing happened."

"That's the least of my concerns, Leo. You want to sleep with other women, fine. Just let me know that the rules have changed. By the way, I like your face. You look good in gauze and tape. Is that why you were in the hospital?"

"Yeah."

"What happened?"

"I got in a fight with a guy. He cut me with a knife. It was bad enough that I had to go to the hospital to get it fixed up. I'm fine now. I won't even have a scar."

"Who was the guy? That woman's pimp? The one we saw at the hospital?"

"Yeah."

"Jesus Christ. I knew it. I know that look on your face."

"Just wait a damn minute. For what it's worth, I didn't do this for vengeance or out of some misguided sense of honor. I wanted some information and taking Jack down was the price. I planned it as well as I could. To do the job and not get caught at it, not by the police or by Jack. I have no interest in doing time or in getting killed. I have too much to live for."

"You could have fooled me."

"Sam, look around us. You can't live scared. You could be blown to hell signing books in a mall bookstore."

"I know that, but you don't have to go looking for trouble."

"I don't."

"The hell you don't. That's your *business*."

"Okay. You're right. That's what I do. But I'm good at it and it's what I like."

"It's just a job, Leo, not a calling. You could quit if you . . ."

"What? If I loved you? Bull. I do love you. I think about you all the time when I'm out there. You're part of the equation for every decision I make. But if I walked away from what I thought was right, I couldn't live with myself. I try to balance that with loving you. I'm really trying to give you equal weight, no more and certainly no less. If you don't feel that, I don't know how to make you see it."

Samantha was silent for quite a while. I kept sneaking glances at her as I drove. Finally, she spoke. "I believe you, Leo, and I'm sure there are ways that you take me into consideration that are invisible to me. I still feel more vulnerable in this relationship. What are you risking with me?"

"Apart from the risks of loving anyone, you mean? How about your fame?"

"My what?"

"You heard me. Oh, I know it's just starting. But it's you doing television interviews and autographings, not me. I'm a nobody, a private eye. The only private eyes anyone's ever heard of are the ones you writers invent: Spade, Marlowe and Archer." Samantha tried to interrupt me. "Yeah, fame and fortune could be yours. You could leave a mark on this culture. Me, my contributions are about as enduring as bubble gum. Wait until you do become famous. It's pretty heady stuff. Next to being idolized, love can look real plain."

"Leo, you can't think that I'm going to run off with the head of my fan club?" She laughed.

"No. I don't. But don't tell me that I'm not risking anything. It's happened before."

"Okay, I hear you. I've honestly never thought about being famous before. I guess I didn't want to be disappointed if it didn't happen."

"It will. Then you can keep me on as your bodyguard." I smiled hopefully.

"You have that job already."

We stopped at a traffic light. Samantha took my chin in her hands, turned my face towards her and gently kissed me. Our tongues negotiated a peace.

"Are we still fighting?" I asked as I stepped on the accelerator.

"I'm not. I have to think about what we've said. I do know that if you die doing something stupidly 'heroic' or whatever you call it, I will never forgive you. Do you understand? Never."

I nodded. "I hear you. Sounds like I'm pretty important to you."

"You want me to put it in writing?"

"Sure. What do you have in mind?"

"How about a great big Technicolor hickey with my name in the center in raised letters?"

"I'm going to hold you to that when we get home."

"Step on it then."

No sooner were we in her apartment than Samantha kicked off her shoes and started to unzip her pants. I watched her silent retreat to the bedroom and then followed, unbuttoning my shirt.

She stepped out of her slacks and kicked them away. Her top followed suit. I kicked off my shoes and unzipped my pants. My eyes were fused to her body. There was an old ache in my chest and my pulse was in my ears. I peeled off my shorts.

We pulled back the cover and slipped underneath it. I rubbed her body as if it were a magic lantern and I had come to free the genie. She responded and our mouths leeched and fed each other. I gently made my way down the left side of her neck. We kissed again and I began to explore her right side. A world of one and world enough for me.

Our need rose like a flood through a canyon. She pulled her legs up and around me like a swan's wings. I entered her and we crashed together with the fit and fury of the surf and the shore. Finally, drained, I rolled over. She rolled with me, unwilling to break the connection. We kissed and rubbed noses. Finally we came apart. After a few minutes I looked over at her. We rolled towards each other and once again I was priest and initiate at her dark altar.

Later I got up to set the clock and sat for a moment watching her. She stirred once in her sleep and smiled briefly. I thought I might sit up all night and watch her but I decided that was crazy and that I'd be of no use to anyone if I didn't get some sleep. I climbed back into bed next to her, reached over and gently cupped her breast as if I were calming a frightened bird. She stirred and I took my hand away. At last, I curled up around her and we slept as close as sleep itself.

Chapter 23

I AWOKE when consciousness filtered in and my groping hands couldn't locate Samantha. I stretched and growled and flung my legs over the side of the bed hoping that, like a kid's punching dummy, my head would snap up behind them. I toddled off to the bathroom, washed the grit out of my eyes with warm water and brushed my teeth. I padded across the living room to the kitchen. As I rounded the corner I stopped to watch her, nude, stretching to put something away. I followed the long line of tensed muscle up her leg and back and, counterpoised, her round uplifted breasts.

"Good morning, sleeping beauty. I've got some breakfast going: scrambled eggs, toast and sausage and some coffee."

I slid into a chair, feasting on her with my eyes, oblivious to everything, even the steaming plate and mug she put in front of me. She bent down and looked me square in the eye. I reached up to touch one of her breasts. She reached down to touch me. We rubbed noses.

"What's this I have here?" she asked. Her eyes widened in mock surprise.

"My seismograph, and it's off the dial. I think we need to evacuate this area."

"A good idea. I'll take some provisions." She put napkin-wrapped silverware on the plates and grabbed them. I took the mugs and we fled.

Much later that morning, I got up again and reached around for my clothes. She was curled up in bed, eyes closed, hugging a pillow. I looked down at her and said, "What are you thinking?"

"I was thinking we can't do this forever, can we?"

"We could try." I kept getting dressed however.

She stood and walked slowly around the bed. I tried to keep dressing but someone had buttered my tie. She went to the bathroom, looked over her shoulder and as she pulled the door closed, winked. I had a double hernia.

When I finished dressing I went into the kitchen and sat down at the dining room table with coffee, my notes and one of Samantha's clean pads. First I wrote a narrative of my last couple of days for my report to Marta Vasquez. Then I went over my notes and made up a list of questions.

Donnelly knew risks. Why mix pills and booze?

Who took the pills, and why?

Who put the note there, and why?

Why did his mood change?

Who was his expert?

I got up, stretched my legs, poured a refill and went over my notes one more time. I compared the dates the record had been signed out and by whom with the entries in the chart. This yielded one more question and a possible answer to them all.

Gutierrez? No entries in chart. Why read it then? Took it out just before Donnelly perked up. Was he his expert?

I needed to see Donnelly's suicide note. Hopefully, Nate had it by now. I arched my back and stretched. Samantha came over, wrapped her arms around my neck, bent over and nibbled on my ear.

"How goes it here?"

"I don't know. I feel like I'm chasing a ghost. I seem to be getting closer to figuring out how Donnelly died, but it feels like there's nothing there. I have him in a room, talking to a doctor, mixing pills and booze — which he knows he shouldn't do — and keeling over dead. Then somebody comes into the room, takes the prescription bottle and leaves a faked suicide note. Why?"

"Maybe the doctor gave him some bad advice on the

phone, came over to check up on him, found him dead, panicked and tried to cover it up?"

"But why get yourself in deeper trouble? At worst we've got malpractice here. But that's a civil matter, an insurance matter."

"What if the doctor had a history of malpractice suits and was in danger of losing his license? Maybe he was afraid he'd lose his livelihood?"

"That's a good point. Maybe I can find out what this doctor's record is with his insurance carrier." I wrote that down on my ever-lengthening list of things to do. I shook my head and put down my pencil. "There's just one problem with this."

Samantha slid around and spilled into my lap. "And what is that?"

"You'd have to be pretty certain Donnelly was dead to show up with a suicide note. If you made an innocent mistake on the phone and went over to check on your patient, you wouldn't carry a typed suicide note with you. You wouldn't expect him to be dead. If you made a mistake on the phone but caught yourself and knew it could be lethal you'd call for an ambulance. The hooker said Donnelly told him the room he was in. Whoever came into that room knew Donnelly would be dead and he brought the note to cover his tracks."

"You're talking about murder."

"I know. A remote control killer and I don't know why."

"Do you know who?"

"Not really. I've got an idea, but I have yet to place him in that room. And I still don't have any motive."

I wrote some more notes for tomorrow. "Samantha, have you ever been in therapy?"

"You mean it isn't obvious?"

"Give me a break. Have you?"

"Yes. Why do you ask?"

"I just might try it out myself and I was wondering if you could give me some pointers on how to be a patient."

"Just be yourself, Leo."

"Ha, ha. I'm serious. I'm thinking about going to see this psychiatrist and I'll need a cover story."

"Okay, I'll tell you what I can. Do you want to do that now?"

"Let me make some calls first. See how they turn out."

I dialed Nate's office. It was answered on the sixth ring.

"Nate Grossbart, please. This is Leo Haggerty."

"So Leo, what do you have for me?" Nate said.

"A question, Nate. Do you have the suicide note there?"

"Yes. Why?"

"I want you to read it to me."

"All right. Hold on." I heard Nate ask his secretary for the Vasquez case, then papers being sorted through. "Here it is, and I quote, 'Can't go on any longer. She's taken my money, my love, my self-respect. Now she's taking my kids. All my plans are a joke. She's outmaneuvered me again. I should have known. Nothing's helping. Drugs. Counseling. No hope. Nothing left to do. No way out. This is on her head. On her head.'"

The note was typical depressive hyperbole. Equal parts rage and hopelessness, shaken not stirred. "Marta Vasquez sure didn't plant that letter. I can see why you'd want an alternative to suicide. No insurance company in their right mind would want to pay a beneficiary who drove the victim to his death."

"So tell me, Leo, what has my money bought me? You have anything to tell me?"

I quickly brought Nate up to date on the case. Give or take a few facts, that is.

"Excellent, Leo. A successful malpractice action is a very acceptable alternative. We'll sue the doctor and the center for a wrongful death. We'll have to pitch the suit on behalf of the children, not the wife, to temper the effects of that letter." Nate was thinking out loud.

"Nate, there's only one problem. I don't think this is malpractice. I think this is murder."

"How did you come to that conclusion?"

I gave Nate my reasoning on the suicide note.

"All of which hinges on the testimony of a thief and a

prostitute. From what you said, she wouldn't pay attention to anything that wasn't negotiable."

"Nate, even if you go the malpractice route, it couldn't have been Truman Whitney."

"And why is that?"

"He was in session with a patient at the time of death and no calls were put through to him. He couldn't have told Malcolm Donnelly that it was okay to drink with the medication in him."

"Again your mystery hooker's story. You said that she only heard Donnelly's side of the conversation, not what this mysterious Doc said. Leo, you don't even have a suspect."

"Yes, I do."

"Who? This Gutierrez?"

"Yes. Nate, he was looking at Donnelly's chart just before he died. Right around the time Donnelly's mood lifted and he said he'd found an expert witness for his custody battle."

"So what? He could have taken the chart out by mistake. You said he hadn't made any notes in the record."

"Nate, whoever wrote that suicide note had to have read the chart. One of the lines is right out of the record."

"Unless Malcolm Donnelly wrote it. I mean, he would know his own mind, wouldn't he?"

"Donnelly wasn't suicidal, goddamnit."

"Says you, Dr. Haggerty. You yourself said that Whitney had doubts about Donnelly's mental status when he terminated treatment. He misdiagnosed the man. He should have hospitalized him. What did he call it, a manic defense? That would jibe with what we saw here. He died because his mental state made him incapable of following the doctor's orders. Whitney should have known that. He wasn't aggressive enough in protecting his patient and he'll have to pay for that. It cost Donnelly his life."

"So that's how you're going to play it, Nate?"

"Damned right. I intend to see that my client and her children do not have to suffer any further financial hardship because of this man's unfortunate mental illness."

"Nate, let me at least check Gutierrez out? See if I can establish opportunity then motive."

"Absolutely not. You have nothing to go on that warrants further expense. I won't have you jeopardizing this case by stumbling around in the dark chasing your phantom killer. I have to stick with legal realities. We have Dr. Whitney's relationship with the patient, a demonstrable breach of the standard of care, clearcut proximate cause and damage—Donnelly's death. All the elements are there and I intend to pursue them."

"Is that what you want, Nate? Just enough to shake something out of the money tree? What it is these days? Do you go to seminars on the lawsuit as an investment form? Greenmail for the little guy. Christ, at least the mob and its kneebreakers are honest about what they're up to."

"I don't have to listen to this, Haggerty. You're off this case. File your report and a final bill. For the record, my job is the vigorous pursuit of my client's legal rights. If you have a beef, it's with the system. I just play by their rules—"

"Save it for Nuremberg, Nate."

"Fuck you, you pigshit Irishman." It was hard to tell who hung up on whom. It took ten minutes for me to calm down enough to make the rest of my calls. Arnie was next on my list.

"Yeah," he said.

"It's Leo, Arnie. Are you going to be home today?"

"Yeah."

"I think it's time we talked. How about I come by around two?"

"Whatever."

"See you then."

I tried to call Dr. Bliss and then Marta Vasquez. Both of their lines were busy. I pulled down the phone book and looked for a Dr. Gutierrez in the district. There was one listed. A Dr. Rolando Gutierrez. I dialed Dr. Rolando Gutierrez's phone number. On the second ring I got a taped message: "This is the office of Dr. Rolando Gutierrez. I am unable to speak with you at this time. At the sound of the tone leave your name, phone number and a brief message."

While I was waiting for the beep, I thought about what

to say and decided to just hang up. I didn't want to give him my real name or phone number. I looked at the clock. It read 11:45. If he observed the fifty-minute hour, I'd call again at 11:50, and try to catch him between sessions. This time he picked up the phone on the first ring.

"Hello, this is Dr. Gutierrez."

"Uh, hello, my name is Francis Jerome. I'd like to make an appointment to see you, Dr. Gutierrez."

"How may I be of assistance to you?" he purred.

"Uh, I'm really not in a position to explain that right now."

"You are not in a private place."

"Yes, that's right."

"Might I ask how you got my name?"

"Uh, that's part of the problem I need to discuss with you, Doc."

"I see. Let me consult my appointment book and see what times are available."

After a brief silence he said, "I have an opening today at four P.M. That's my last appointment today. Is that convenient for you?"

"Oh, yes, that's fine. No problem."

"Good. We'll talk and see if I can be of any help to you. Do you have my office address?"

"Yes."

"Fine. The door to the office is in the back of the house. Walk through the garden and I will meet you there at four P.M."

"Uh, one last question. How much does a session cost?"

"My regular fee is eighty-five dollars per session. However, there is no charge for the initial consultation. That is so we can freely get acquainted and see if we can work together. Until then."

I called Dr. Bliss again and this time I got through. He politely told me he was no longer free to discuss the Donnelly case. I went ahead and called Marta Vasquez even though I wasn't optimistic about what she would have to say.

"Hello, this is Leo Haggerty."

"Oh hello, Mr. Haggerty."

"I'd like to talk to you about your husband's death, if I may."

"I'm sorry Mr. Haggerty, my lawyer has advised me not to discuss this matter with you any further."

"Don't you care about what really happened to your husband? I think he was murdered!"

"I'm sorry, Mr. Haggerty, my attorney has told me about your speculations and about the evidence against Dr. Whitney. I'm inclined to believe Mr. Grossbart, that this was a case of malpractice, and I'm satisfied that that is the truth. I have no idea why you would pursue this other idea. I cannot imagine why this other doctor would want to kill Malcolm. From what Mr. Grossbart said, they'd never even met."

"Mrs. Vasquez, Marta—"

"I'm sorry, that's all I have to say on this matter."

The click in my ear left me wondering what I'd done to Truman Whitney and how to let him know that the shit and the fan were very close indeed.

Samantha trotted by on the way to her desk and another day at the paper mill.

"Samantha, I'm off to see Randi Benson and then Arnie. How about I swing by here after that and get that lecture on how to be a psychotherapy patient?"

"Okay."

"By the way, Nate fired me."

"Why?"

"A little disagreement over legal philosophies, that's all."

"Right. So why are you keeping at this thing?"

"Because I think Nate's going to scapegoat an innocent man and because Gutierrez just might be a murderer. Without Wanda Manlove's testimony about the pills, and the letter, Nate will have a pretty easy time making this out to be a wrongful death."

"Your evidence is mighty slim, you know."

"I know. I'll give this a couple of days, though. At least until Marta Vasquez orders me to stop the investigation in writing. After that, I'd be risking a review board hearing by keeping at it, and I like to eat."

"Okay. I'll be here all afternoon."

"Do you have class tonight?"

"Yeah, but I have to go in early. There's a faculty meeting. How about I come by your place after class?"

"Do that." I went to the closet to get my jacket. Samantha slipped her headphones on. "Damn," she said.

"What's the matter?"

"There's a short in my stereo. It keeps cutting out."

"Let me look at it." I reached under her tuner and felt for a loose connection. Having found one, I wiggled it into place and admonished the tuner to turn its head and cough. The system came to life.

"Thanks, stranger."

" 'Twarn't nothin', ma'am." I bent down and we kissed.

"Leo. Humor me. Use back roads and small shops. And remember three's a crowd."

"I hear you. You be careful too."

A half hour later I was tromping across the parking lot of the private school Randi Benson attended. She was sitting on the front steps of the administration building, waiting for me.

"Hi," I said. "Do I have to sign in or anything?"

"No. I told my guidance counselor you were coming. So she signed me out."

"How's school going? I got your last report card." I wanted to stay neutral about her grades.

"What did you think?"

No such luck. "Randi, I don't care about your grades. What I care about is if you're happy. Are you happy?"

"I'm getting there. Did I tell you that I'm on the school literary magazine now? I want to ask Samantha if she'll come out and talk to us."

"I'm sure she'd be delighted." We were dancing around a dead moose. "How's Tammy doing?" Tammy was her eight-year-old sister. The court order covered her too.

"She's doing great. She's going to be in the gifted and talented program next year."

I stroked my mustache. "You wanted to talk about your dad, remember?"

She turned away and then back again. Her blond hair was now cropped short and she wore much less makeup than when I first knew her. At fourteen, she looked a lot better in plaid skirts and penny loafers than she had in a garter belt and spike heels.

"He's pressuring my mother again. He wants us home for Thanksgiving, so we'll look like a family. He wants her to make us come home. She's called here three times this week and she was drunk each time. She cries and tells us she can't go on like this. Tammy says she wants to go home for Thanksgiving. Her therapist says it's okay."

"What do you want to do?"

"I don't want to go back there. Tammy's at me to come home with her. I don't want to leave her alone there, but I just can't stand being in that house."

"What do you want me to do?"

She drew lines on the the sidewalk with the toe of her shoe. "I don't know."

"I know you, kiddo. When you start feeling trapped you start lacing up your track shoes. You're getting ready to bolt, aren't you?"

"Yeah. I guess. That's why I called. I could feel it coming on. The last time I ran, I got in a lot of trouble. I'm afraid I'll do it again."

"I'll tell you what. I don't think you should go to your father's for Thanksgiving. In fact, I forbid it. Since I'm your legal guardian, I can do that. It's not up to you. I don't care what you want to do. In fact, I'll tell him that today."

"Would you?" She'd brightened up considerably.

"Sure. Is there anything else?"

"Nah. I guess not."

"Okay. You want to walk me back to my car?"

"Sure. Then I'll have to take off to science class."

We walked together across the campus. At my car I turned and said, "Oh, by the way, there's one other reason why you can't go there for Thanksgiving."

"Oh, what's that?" she asked disinterestedly.

"You'll be celebrating it with me and Samantha. That is, if you want to."

"All right!" She strung out the syllables as far as they would go. "Thank you. That's great. I was hoping I could but I was afraid to ask."

"You shouldn't have to. I'm sorry I waited so long to let you know." I unlocked my car, slid in and rolled down the window. Randi gave me a quick peck on the cheek, waved good-bye and took off across the lawn at a gallop. A couple of times she jumped into the air and shook her fist at the sky. Watching her disappear into the school I felt a warm glow in my chest and the beginnings of a smile on my face. It was still strange to be that important to another person.

It was just shy of two when I pulled up at Arnie's house. I sat in the car wondering how this was going to turn out. Arnie had sounded pretty listless on the phone, maybe depressed even. My feelings flickered unstably between anger and concern, and I wasn't the least bit sure that either one was going to be of any use here. I climbed out of the car, slammed the door shut and trudged up to his house.

The front door was open, so I walked right in. Arnie slouched, unshaven, in the same chair I'd seen him in a couple of days ago. The pile around him was noticeably higher. He ran his fingers through his hair so that it stood up wildly, and glowered at me without conviction.

"What do you want?"

"Just came by to see how you were doing."

"Well, you've seen. Is that it?" he sneered.

"No, asshole, that's not it. What's the matter? A little caring too much for you to deal with? Doesn't fit in with your godalmighty code? What are you afraid of? That you might start caring for other people, too? Let me tell you something, your *bushido* bullshit only works if you keep it simple. Care for no one but yourself, loyalty to no one but yourself and it works fine. Let somebody else get close to you, start having to take them into account and things don't sort out so nice, do they? What is it that your teacher says? 'The hand that is always clenched is full with its own emptiness.' " Nice work, Haggerty, when in doubt, get pissed off. Was I really treating Samantha any better than this?

"You think I want to be out here all by myself?" Arnie's tone and eyes had softened.

"Sure looks that way to me."

"Do you have any idea how much I've wanted to come home? I left 'Nam behind; that's not it. I just never could arrive in America."

"Was going to the wall part of this?"

"Yeah, that's part of it. Being recognized finally, being welcomed back finally. I really thought that I'd feel better after I went down there. But it's just not okay. I just can't do it. I can't slide back in like the last fifteen years never happened. I've changed too much. It's too little and it's too late for me."

I sat down on the side table next to Arnie's chair. "I hear you. I'm not saying that you have to forget what happened. But you don't have to stay out in the cold. The door is open, Arnie, walk through it. Come on home."

"I can't. I just can't." He held his head in his hands.

I put my hand on his shoulder. "Try. I'll walk it with you."

Arnie just sat there shaking his head. Next to him, I was not at all sure where we went from here.

Chapter 24

I KNOCKED on the door to Samantha's apartment. She pulled it open, saw that it was me and turned away saying, "Come on in."

I cocked an eyebrow, said, "Now what" to myself and walked in. She walked over and plopped down on her sofa. She balanced a glass on her chest and had a frown stamped on her face.

"Why so glum? What happened?"

"Nothing." She tried to take a sip from her glass but the angle was all wrong. Grumbling, she sat up.

"Nothing, my ass. What is it?"

She took a sip from the glass and handed me a magazine. It was folded back to a review of her latest book. I skimmed it until I came to the cause of death: "the vastly overpraised Ms. Clayton, whose previous volume was short-listed for a number of literary prizes, repeatedly offers us character-ization by quirk, and not surprisingly, none of her 'shtick figures' rouses any genuine feelings."

"Whew." I dropped the magazine like it was radioactive.

"Witty son-of-a-bitch, isn't he?"

"You want I should take him out?" I said in my best nasal, thick-tongued Brooklynese.

"No. I don't want you to be funny either."

"Okay." I dropped the accent as if it was the magazine. "Hurts, huh?"

She took a big slug from the glass. "Damn right it does. Oh by the way, Mrs. Murphy, why didn't you drown that child? It's not very pretty, you know."

"Ah, fuck 'em. Them that can, do, them that can't criticize."

"I'll get over the hurt. Everybody gets trashed, right? It's just one person's opinion, right?"

"Absolutely. Nothing a good review can't fix."

"To hell with reviews. If you want to believe the good ones, then you have to believe the bad ones too. I just wish that I didn't give a damn. That I could write just for myself."

"No, you don't. Then you'd have to keep it all in a drawer."

"True. I'm just as angry with myself. I guess I have to accept that I'm not immune to criticism."

"Just as long as you don't let it determine what you write."

"No way. You know what really burns me up though?"

"No. What?"

"Being the butt of his little jokes. 'Shtick figures,'" she sneered. "If he wants to criticize my work, fine. There's no reason to ridicule it though. That's a cheap shot. If he's so fucking funny, how come I haven't read anything of his between covers?"

"I'll ask him that, right before I let him have it." I watched to see if there was even the hint of a smile on her face. Finally it began to peek through.

"On second thought, how much does it cost to do in a third-rate book reviewer?"

"Depends on how you want it done. The cheapest way is to make him eat his words until he chokes on them."

"I like that. You're hired."

"Fine. One problem though. I have a therapy appointment to get to first. Can you give me any pointers on how to be mentally ill?"

"For you? Just one."

"Okay, shoot. What is it?"

"Act naturally." Her smile was in full bloom now.

I mimed putting a gun in my mouth and pulling the trigger. "Seriously though, any tips before I go see this guy?"

"I don't know. You need to have a problem to talk about. That's why you're there."

"You mean other than why did you kill Malcolm Donnelly?"

"You catch on quick. Whatever story you use ought to be something you're familiar with. You'll sound more believable that way. If you don't want to talk much about yourself, act paranoid, try to interview him instead. Tell him that you're therapist shopping. Remember that if he's any good he'll follow you for a while, listening to you tell your story and then he'll try to take you and it someplace new. A good therapist does the unexpected, asks the questions you never ask yourself, challenges what you assume to be true. If he's any good you'd better be on your toes."

"Point well taken. See you after class." I looked at my watch. "I'd better be going. Isn't it supposed to mean something if you're late for your appointment?"

"Shoo. I have work to do."

I took 395 North towards the Pentagon. The Washington Boulevard exit took me right past it. Fifteen years ago they had had machine guns in the halls to repel "invaders." Meanwhile, a hundred thousand such "invaders" were marching downtown intent on putting sugar in the war machine's gas tank.

The sidewalks near the Arlington National Cemetery were empty. No more afternoon runs for the military staff. One bomb on the bridge and half the colonels we have would be floating in the Potomac. The Iwo Jima Memorial was on my left as I entered Rosslyn to take Key Bridge into Georgetown.

In Georgetown, I turned left away from the commercial strip along M Street and headed towards the residential areas around the university. I found Dr. Gutierrez's address and parked half a block down from it. I locked the car and walked towards his house. It was narrow, deep and three stories high. The brick was painted an odd gray-blue color. On the first two floors all the windows had ornate metal grillwork over them as did the door. There was a fence around the property made of the same curved ironwork. A slate path went between the house and a row of thorny plants that ran up a trellis above the fence.

As I walked towards the house I could see that the same grillwork covered the windows on the side of the house and that the basement window wells were also enclosed by a metal grill. When I got to the back of the house I reminded myself to think like a patient. I was here to get a reading on the man and I needed to be as believable and unremarkable as possible. I was having trouble, however, turning off my vigilance so that I could focus on creating a problem. The fence and trellis continued around the back of the house. There were no tables or chairs out. Nothing to enjoy the brick patio. Only two high-intensity floodlights mounted at the corners of the back wall of the house. I looked at the door to the doctor's office. There was no brass nameplate there. Nothing at all to identify it as a doctor's office.

I rang the doorbell and shifted from foot to foot waiting for the door to open. A man pulled the door back slowly, smoothly. He was slight, much smaller than me. His hair was thick, jet black and combed straight back from his high forehead. A bushy mustache lay across his upper lip like a furry caterpillar.

"Yes," he said softly.

"Uh, Dr. Gutierrez?"

"Yes, I am Dr. Gutierrez." He looked directly at me with dark brown eyes, made somewhat larger by the thick glasses he wore.

"Uh, I'm Mr. Jerome. Francis Jerome. I spoke with you earlier."

"Yes, Mr. Jerome. Please come in." With that he extended his hand and I shook it. But for a large signet ring, his grip was as sleek and soft as a seal's flipper. He turned his back to me and said, "Please follow me." Gutierrez wore a navy blue sweater, gray wool slacks, and high gloss black shoes. I followed him down a dark corridor towards a staircase. We descended the staircase. At the bottom Gutierrez reached for a doorknob on the right, pushed it open, and motioned for me to enter.

"Please sit there, Mr. Jerome."

I sat in a chocolate leather recliner. "Thank you," I said. There were two recliners in the room and they were angled towards each other. Between them stood a small table with Dr. Gutierrez's pipes and other smoking paraphernalia. The carpet was cocoa colored and the walls almost taupe. A desk stood against the far wall. The only interesting thing on it was his typewriter. The lighting was recessed and indirect. Everything about the room seemed muted. Gutierrez closed the door and walked to his chair. I scanned the room and found there was nothing to distract one's gaze. Nothing to look at but the doctor. I reminded myself I was just here to get a reading on the man. To see if I could trip him up. Get him to give himself away.

"You look very tense, Mr. Jerome." Gutierrez was in his seat, legs crossed, one hand propping up his head.

"Yeah, well like I, uh, said, I've never done this before." I needed to get a grip on this.

"Oh? You didn't say that on the phone," he said with a smile.

"I didn't? Well I thought I did. I don't remember much of what I said. I couldn't talk freely."

"Yes, you did say that." Gutierrez shifted from the left to the right side of his chair.

"Is everything we say here confidential?"

"Absolutely, Mr. Jerome. In fact, the walls and ceiling are soundproofed. No one can hear you in here."

I looked around for something to talk about. "Do you keep notes of what we say? I don't see any records. Are you taping me?"

"No, Mr. Jerome. I assure you I am not taping you. My records are kept in my desk under lock and key for my patients' protection. You seem quite suspicious, Mr. Jerome. Very much on guard."

"No. No, I'm not. Uh, I'm just not used to doing this sort of thing."

"May I ask how you got my name, Mr. Jerome?"

"Uh, a friend of mine told me about you. Malcolm Donnelly." I met his gaze head-on. No reaction. Absolutely none. If I was right about this guy, he was very good. He'd probably 'flatline' a lie detector.

"I see. It was a tragedy about Malcolm. To die by one's

own hand. To find life so unbearable. A great shame. I am sorry you have lost a friend. That is a tragedy in itself."

"Uh, yes. Thank you."

"Let me be frank with you, Mr. Jerome. If any of your distress is at all due to Mr. Donnelly's death I'm not sure we should work together."

"Really? Why not?" This was like picking up mercury with mittens on.

"I have had to ask myself many times whether I misdiagnosed Mr. Donnelly. It weighs heavily on me." Gutierrez looked away for a moment. "He consulted me about a domestic matter and I felt I might be of some assistance to him. I fear I misjudged the depth of his despair, his sense of hopelessness."

Gutierrez looked back at me. "If your being here is at all due to Malcolm's death, I don't think I would be able to assist you in your own personal explorations of that without being partially concerned with protecting myself from feelings of guilt brought on by your quite legitimate anger and hurt. There is no room for such self-serving in the therapeutic relationship. Do you see what I am driving at?" He looked at me earnestly.

"Uh, yes. No, that's not why I'm here. Malcolm and I weren't that close. I just got your name from him. That's all."

"Well then, Mr. Jerome, what does bring you here?"

Time to put up or shut up. "Uh, well, it's really . . ." My mind was spinning while the room stood still. It was hard to remember why I had come.

"I can't, uh, seem to remember things. Like when I forgot what I said on the phone to you."

"You remember that?"

"Yeah, yeah, it's not things like that I forget. I mean, I did forget that, but that's not what I'm concerned about." I looked up at Gutierrez. He sat there, calmly, silently. Then he leaned back away from me.

I had the oddest feeling that we were somehow breathing together, somehow tethered to each other. I felt the push and pull, yet for the life of me I could not see where we were joined.

"It's mostly before age five that I can't remember."

"You say mostly. So you can remember some things that occurred before age five?"

"Yes, yes."

"You remember that by age five, you no longer forgot to remember things?"

"I guess so." The vortex deepened, got narrower, darker. I spun faster. This is getting out of hand. I didn't come here to get therapy. This is just pretend. If I leave now he'll think I'm a real flake. What do I care?

"You're concerned about recovering your childhood?"

"Yeah, I guess that's it." Get a grip on this. Direct it somewhere. Make up something. Every time I reached down into my imagination for a diversion I flung up a piece of myself that fluttered and fell like a wounded bird. Imagination's shadow is the flesh and there is no escaping that. I spun on madly, trying to flee anyway.

"Close your eyes, Mr. Jerome. What did you lose when you were five?" The room grew darker. I thought I saw Dr. Gutierrez turn a dial on his chair.

"I don't know. I can't remember." A dorsal fin broke the smooth surface of my forgetting.

"Maybe it's better if you forgot."

"No. I don't want to forget. That's why I came here." Get out of here, man. I saw an empty crib. A sour bile rose in my throat. Shame's dessert.

"Sometimes the mind works that way, Mr. Jerome. Everything is remembering and forgetting. Forgetting to remember. Remembering to forget. Always when you want to. Sometimes you must forget things . . ."

"But I can't forget . . ." My heart was pounding. I felt my palms. They were slick with fear and shame.

"That is good, Mr. Jerome. Now you can remember what you forgot."

"Um, Dr. Gutierrez, I can't seem to remember why I came here. I feel really foolish about this, but I think I'm going to have to leave early . . ." I stood up, barely able to keep from running.

Dr. Gutierrez stood up, and pointed to the small clock behind my chair. "Actually, our time is up. You are a very interesting person, Mr. Jerome. Think about our session. If you would like to enter psychotherapy I believe I could be of tremendous help to you. Certain hypnotic techniques might help unlock those repressed memories. You seem quite responsive to trance induction."

He moved towards the door. "Let me show you out. I must prepare for a meeting this evening. Good day, Mr. Jerome."

I shook his hand and slid past him. I felt deeply ashamed and did not know why.

On the street, I looked left and right and crossed quickly towards my car. My mind was overflowing. Questions spilled everywhere. What memory lurked just beyond reach? Why was I so ashamed? How had Gutierrez been able to control me so easily? Behind them I felt, once again, the panic I had known in that room. The fear that my mind was not my own.

I climbed into my car and drove off, more uncertain than ever about Dr. Gutierrez and the death of Malcolm Donnelly. Halfway home I remembered that I'd forgotten to stay and take his picture to show to the hotel staff.

Chapter 25

I WENT HOME to an empty house. My appetite was nowhere to be found either. I decided on two pain pills for dinner. Those I washed down with some beer. I knew I shouldn't mix them, but I didn't really care. I even tried to summon up some curiosity about my indifference but failed.

The session with Gutierrez had disoriented me. I knew I should try to figure out what had happened and what it meant, but as I watched my feet lead me into my office I also knew that, truth be told, I was afraid of the answers.

My desk provided me with some unpleasant but welcome distractions. I typed out a final report for Nate Grossbart, Xeroxed it and my expense log and sealed them in an envelope. The copies went into my files. Then I stared at the note I had taped to my lamp: Call Benson. I would rather have my teeth pulled. Leaning back in my chair, I dialed his house. Sadly, I knew the number by heart.

"Hello, Tillie. This is Leo Haggerty. Is Mr. Benson there?"

Tillie was silent for quite a while. "I'll get him for you. Hold on please."

The phone erupted in my ear with Benson yelling, "What the fuck do you want, Haggerty? How dare you call me at my home!"

I had learned through hard experience over the last year to ignore most of Benson's insults and accusations and to stick to the facts, just the facts.

"Randi will not be coming home for Thanksgiving."

"Why the hell not?" he bellowed.

"Because I say so."

"You can't do that, you son of a bitch."

"The hell I can't. I'm her legal guardian, and what I say goes. It's as simple as that."

"You can't block visitation forever, you know. I have rights. She has to see me sometimes."

"When I say so. And don't call me or her. I'll call you. In fact, the next time you or your wife call her I'm going to delay visitation another month."

"Fuck you, Haggerty. You scumbag. You better watch your step. Maybe I'll put a peeper on you. Watch you 'round the clock for a while, see what kind of 'moral atmosphere' you provide for a teenaged girl. It can go both ways, you know."

"You're welcome to try. You might want to use Carmine Nicoletti, he's your kind of guy. You want the number?"

I took the resounding crash of the receiver for a no. There were no other loose ends I could distract myself with so I went into the living room and turned on the television. Somewhere along the way, helped no doubt by the beer and the pills, the somnolent effects of canned laughter and inane dialogue overcame me and I fell asleep. The last afterimages from the television died away and became dream images.

There was a ball lying alongside some railroad tracks I was following. I looked behind me and the tracks were lost in the distance. Ahead, they disappeared in the shimmering desert air. I couldn't recall why I was following these tracks and decided that it would be more fun to play ball than march on. I kicked the ball away from the tracks and began to follow it. I followed the ball across the desert and kicked it into a room. As I ran towards the room its heavy door swung closed. I ran right up to it and saw that there was no handle to the door. I felt all over it for a way in. I wanted my ball back. I started to kick the door, but it did no good. Suddenly there was a man standing next to me. He was so tall that I couldn't see his face. As he reached out to the door, a doorknob emerged from the wood and slipped easily into his hand. He turned the knob and let me into the room. I ran by him. My ball was on the floor next to a crib. I bent down and picked it up. There was a baby in the crib. It was a girl, my sister. She was blue, which was funny, because she should be pink. Actually, I was glad she was blue. Now she was like me. But my mother really liked her because she was pink. I figured I'd better get out of here, because they'll think I turned her blue. But I didn't. She was just like that when I found her. I ran back to the door. It was closed. I didn't hear it swing shut behind me. I reached up to grab the doorknob but it wouldn't turn. It was very slippery. I dropped my ball to try with both hands, but it was no good. I couldn't turn the knob and I couldn't get out. Someone was laughing at me. I looked between my hands and saw the doorknob turn into a face. It was laughing at me and its spittle was flying all over me. Everywhere it touched me I was burning. I looked at the knob and the face was Rolando Gutierrez's and his laughter burned me. My face burned.

"Leo. Leo, are you okay? Say something," I heard a voice say. I blinked once, then again. My heart was in my mouth. I tried to swallow and force it back into my chest. It was still dark, but there was no door in front of me. I blinked again.

"I'm okay. I was having a nightmare." In the dark, I felt squeezed down to a pinpoint, and a loathsome one at that. As my night vision returned, the pinpoint spread out and like a kaleidoscope, other colors emerged, formed, dissolved and reformed. Eventually I looked up and saw Samantha's face. There were furrows in her forehead. The start of a frown held in abeyance by the tentative smile at the corners of her mouth. She looked glad that I was back but worried about where I'd been.

"Whew. That really freaked me out." I ran the back of my hand across my face.

"Here, wait. Let me get you something."

"Okay."

Samantha got off the sofa and hurried to the bathroom. When she returned, she held up my chin and swabbed my face with a cool washcloth. I closed my eyes. I still felt flushed. Finally my heart stopped pounding. I took a deep breath to try to calm myself down.

"Do you want to tell me about it?"

"Whew. Thanks. Yeah, I guess so. I think it all started when I went and saw that shrink, Gutierrez, today. The session didn't go at all like I expected it would. Somehow he took control of the session and I started to feel very strange, very weird."

"How so?"

"It felt like no matter which way I moved my mind to evade him, he anticipated each move, countered it, and was herding me towards things I didn't want to talk about."

"Did you go there pretending to be a patient?"

"Yeah, and that's what's really confusing about the whole thing. Gutierrez was just doing his job, I guess. He seemed genuinely concerned about Donnelly and about me. I don't know though. The more he outmaneuvered me, the more confused and the more frightened I got."

"What finally happened?"

"I just told him that I was going to leave. I'd changed my mind. So I up and left. He said something about being able to help me with hypnosis, that I went into trance easily."

"Do you think he hypnotized you?"

"I don't know. I've never been hypnotized that I can remember. If he did, I don't know how he did it. No swinging watches. No 'when I count three, you will do as I say.' This wasn't the stage magician brand of hypnosis. I sure as hell felt out of control though."

Samantha squeezed my hand, "Do you want to tell me about the dream?"

"Yeah. I think it was a dream about my sister Caitlin."

"Your sister? I didn't know you had a sister."

"I don't. She died when she was about eight months old. Crib death, they called it. A total mystery. No explanation. Just boom, you're dead. No reason."

"How old were you when this happened?"

"Probably three and a half when she died. I think this

was what I was starting to remember when I was with Gutierrez—her death. What really undid me was that I felt so ashamed, and I didn't know why. I just knew that if I stayed in that room with him I was going to start crying and telling him things I didn't want to, so I left."

"What were you ashamed of? Do you know now?"

"I think I do. When I was in the room looking at her in the crib, I remembered that a part of me was glad that she was dead. I hadn't wanted a sister. I didn't want to share things with anyone."

"Have you ever told this to anyone?"

"Not hardly. I didn't even realize it until the dream. I mean, I knew my sister had died, but not that I had been glad. Somehow I kept that hidden until now. I think Gutierrez somehow drove me out of my hiding places. That's not fair though. I wanted to stop hiding as much as I wanted to hide. He just kept finding ways to remind me that I wanted to remember until that was all I wanted to do. Tonight it just all bubbled up in my mind. It's still hard to accept that I could feel that way towards her. She was my sister. I mean, I remember playing with her, too, and helping to take care of her with my mother."

"Leo, you were three years old and wishes aren't deeds."

"Maybe. It's just not the way I like to think of myself. Protector of the innocent and all that crap, and here I am glad that my sister is dead. Not real pretty."

"But real human, Leo. Look at me." She held my hands. "What use would I have for a saint, or he for me?"

"How many guesses do I get?"

"One. So make it count." With that, I let her lead me away from my disillusionment. It would be easy enough to find again should I want to.

"You know what, Leo Jerome Haggerty?"

"No. What?"

"I think I love you, that's what."

I picked her up in my arms and carried her to the bedroom. Sam kicked off one shoe, then the next. They caromed off the hall wall. I kicked open the door. We fell on the bed, and, fumble-fingered, tried to undress each other. Some mending would be necessary. She ran her fingers through my hair and pulled our faces together. Our tongues began the slinky flow of need between us. She would lead. I would follow. Back and forth, we wove ourselves on the loom of sex into the fabric of each other's flesh. We climbed an ever-steeper staircase and leaped through a window. I flew. I fell. Icarus landing with a smile on the warm cheek of a woman. Samantha rolled me onto my back and ministered to my retreating desire. The kiss of life. A Lazarus of the loins. Mounted, happy is the steed. We rode on ever faster. She strummed herself and then dug her fingers into my chest. Eyes closed, she arched until her back would break. Finally the bow snapped and she was released. She shuddered and draped herself limply across me. I held her tightly. At least briefly we were out of harm's way.

She nuzzled my neck. "Umm. You are just what I wanted. Just what I need."

I smiled all the way through. "Do tell?"

"God, an ounce of abandon is worth a ton of technique."

"You mean my variable speed tongue with reverse and overdrive isn't what does it?"

"No, darling. It's your desire, your passion, that I want. I can diddle myself just fine, but I don't hunger for myself. Never have."

With that we began again and chased, caught and released each other from our prisons of desire until there was nowhere left to go.

Chapter 26

SAMANTHA STUCK HER HEAD IN while I was shaving.

"Breakfast is on. Come and get it."

"On my way."

I dried off, put on a robe and went into the kitchen. Samantha had really laid out a spread. Eggs over easy on a pile of corned beef hash, English muffins with butter and raspberry jam and freshly ground coffee.

Samantha sat down with just a muffin and coffee. She flipped through the paper, parceling out what we were each interested in. I got sports, national and metro news. She took food, show and style. The rest was debris. The picture of the man they suspected of being the "memorial bomber" was on the front page. I spent a few minutes staring at it. Halfway down the page from it was a photograph of General Villarosa, due to arrive today. His famous profile was shown to good advantage. While I chased the last remnants of hash around my plate, I watched Samantha devour an article on Caribbean hideaways.

"You know, I've been thinking about my dream. Why was Gutierrez's head on the doorknob? Why was he laughing? It doesn't square with the rest of the dream."

Samantha looked up. "No, it doesn't. He sounds like he was just doing his job and that he's damn good at it."

"Tell me about it. His gentleness seemed real enough. And you're right, he was doing his job. He found my private pain. That's what he was supposed to do. I was the one there under false pretenses. I just can't shake the feeling that he was gloating, though. That he enjoyed watching me squirm."

"In the dream or in the session?"

"Clearly in the dream. He had me where he wanted me. I couldn't get out. I just don't believe that I made that up for no reason. I must have sensed something in that room that I couldn't articulate but it came back to me as part of the dream. I don't think I can ignore it."

"So run a background check on him. You've got your personal impressions of him. See where he fits in his professional community."

"Very good, Watson, I shall."

With that I went into my office and let my fingers do the walking. An hour later I knew that Dr. Rolando Gutierrez had no hospital or teaching affiliations in the area. I went back to the kitchen and poured out the dregs of the coffee. Samantha walked in fully dressed and said, "Got to go." She gave me a light kiss. "I'm going over to Sandra's. She's asked me to read her first draft and tell her what I think. We'll probably go out to eat, stay up late and talk. Call me tomorrow."

"Sure. Oh, by the way, you might want to give Arnie a call. I went by to see him again. He's hurting bad, and he's real stuck. I don't know whether he needs to be cut loose or reeled in."

"Okay. I'd be glad to. How long do you think you'll pursue this loose end?"

"Today, maybe tomorrow. I'd hate to be the one to give Truman Whitney over to Nate. I know Malcolm consulted with Gutierrez. I'd bet he was the one Donnelly called when he was in the hotel room. I'll never be able to prove that though. If I can put him in the hotel, that'll help. The suicide note had a verbatim line from Donnelly's chart. Only Gutierrez and Whitney signed that chart out, and I can account for Whitney."

Even as I said that my noose turned to smoke. I remembered that anybody could read the chart, provided they didn't leave the records room. Maybe looking into Gutierrez's background would turn something up. "Even if Donnelly's death isn't murder, Gutierrez has something pretty big to cover up. If I had a patient I was worried about, I don't think I'd sit down first to type out a suicide note, a carefully worded suicide note. Not unless I was awfully worried about something being discovered. I'm going to follow up your idea about his insurance coverage, but if that's not it, then what is it? If he murdered Donnelly that's big enough to cover up, but for the life of me I don't know why. It also doesn't square with my feelings about Gutierrez. He seemed genuinely warm and concerned when I talked to him."

"But you also dreamt of him as a laughing doorknob that kept you locked in a room with a lot of pain."

"Maybe that was just resentment at him for doing his job?"

"Maybe not. Maybe it's your unconscious telling you not to ignore all these questions. Anyway, now that I've sent the manuscript back to my publisher, I thought we might sneak away for a few days."

"Now there's an idea."

"I have a new crop and some spurs I've been dying to break in." She laughed.

"Dream on. I never met a rider who couldn't be throwed."

"Nor I the horse that couldn't be rode."

"Isn't that us in a nutshell." We kissed again. "Be careful. Remember, there are no smart bombs."

Back at my desk, I started calling the local and national professional associations. Another hour later and Dr. Rolando Gutierrez remained a mystery. There were no collegial ties, no professional oversights, no rudder nor helmsman to help him steer a course in the mainstream of his craft. Nothing but a soundproofed room in a house without a nameplate. He was a psychiatric UFO. No radar blips, no pictures, no debris left behind. If I hadn't had a close encounter I wouldn't have believed in him.

All the information I had sought so far was about optional affiliations. Time to go back to basics. Like myself, he had to have a license to practice and malpractice insurance. Skill or talent are optional. I called the local licensing board.

"Hello. Licenses. Moultrie speaking."

"How do you do, Mr. Moultrie. This is Carl Rivington, over at C.M.H.C. We've had an insurance reimbursement claim denied against Dr. Rolando Gutierrez. Seems he failed to list his license number on the claim. Could you give me that number so we can expedite this. Dr. Gutierrez is out of town right now and there's quite a large amount of money outstanding."

"No problem. Hold on, please."

I sat there waiting to see if Dr. Gutierrez was real in the eyes of anyone other than me.

"Dr. Rolando Gutierrez holds license number 3431."

"Thank you. Does he have any specialty areas listed on his license?"

"Why do you need that?"

"We are conducting a review of all professional staff. Considering the cost of our liability insurance we want to be sure no one is working outside of his area of competence. I just thought I'd kill two birds with one stone, as long as you have his file there."

"Okay, his specialty areas are cross cultural psychiatry, and hypnotherapy."

"Could you tell me where he received his training?"

"The Instituto de Psicologica."

The what? "Excuse me, where is that located?"

"Buenos Aires."

"Thank you." Bingo. I may not have you in that room yet, but I've got you and Malcolm on the same planet at least. I made another call.

"National Psychiatric Association."

"Hello, I'm a newly licensed psychiatrist and I'd like to know who handles the profession's malpractice insurance."

"I'll connect you with the insurance office."

"Thank you."

"Insurance. Mrs. Pendleton. May I help you?"

"Yes. Who is the profession's liability carrier? I'm interested in getting coverage since I'm going into private practice."

"The carrier is National Medical Liability Underwriters."

"Are they the only company that offers coverage for psychiatrists?"

"No, but they are the association's carrier and our group policy rates would be quite a bit lower than any individual coverage you could obtain."

"Is there another carrier?"

"Well, yes. Diversified Risk is now offering a policy on an individual basis. They're testing the market. If there is a response, they'll make us a competitive bid next year." She sounded miffed that I'd even consider that option.

"Thank you. You've been very helpful." I knew that Gutierrez wasn't an association member so he couldn't be under their group policy. I called Diversified Risk.

"Diversified Risk Insurance Company. How may I help you?"

"I'm interested in taking out a liability insurance policy. I'm a psychiatrist."

"Hold on. That's Mr. Drummond's contract." She put me through to him.

I went through my spiel one more time. Drummond asked how I'd found out about the policy they were offering.

"A friend of mine, Rolando Gutierrez, told me about it." There was a silence on the line.

"That's funny, we've just begun to sell that policy in this area and I handle all the contracts. I don't recognize the name. Anyway, what kind of coverage were you looking for?"

I droned on about what I wanted but I wasn't listening to Drummond. After he told me he'd send me an application, I thanked him and hung up. Gutierrez wasn't concerned about prior malpractice claims. He was going bareback. Taking his chances on nothing going wrong. That would put him in even greater risk. He'd have to pay any judgment against him out of his own pocket. Maybe that was enough incentive to sit down at his typewriter before he left to see Donnelly. Maybe they knew each other in Argentina and Gutierrez offered to do Donnelly a favor. But Donnelly said he'd found an expert who could say that Marta was unfit. Gutierrez's specialties did not include forensic work.

That didn't sound too ethical but maybe it was just Donnelly's adrenaline talking or mania as Whitney thought. My loose ends were fraying rapidly.

I sat and doodled for a while. When I had started to run my business out of my house I'd had to make changes in my homeowner's insurance coverage. I'd needed special premises liability coverage for the client who slipped on the icy driveway and so on. I couldn't get that without a zoning change on my residential use permit. They'd come in and inspected the structural changes I'd made, like the safe installed in the floor slab. I'd been pretty keen about getting this done by the book. Otherwise, my homeowner's policy would have been void and I'd have been liable for the replacement cost of the house. For the hell of it I called the zoning office.

"Zoning. Harcourt Bryce speaking."

"Yeah. Well, this is Tony Petrillo, Petrillo Plumbing. I'm over here at Dr. Gutierrez's place. We're ready to make those changes for that office in his house and the building permits ain't here. Nothin' is. This is costing me money sitting around here. The doc says he filed everything with you people. You think you could let us know when the paperwork will be done so we can get to work here?"

"What was that address?"

I gave Bryce the address and waited while he punched it into his computer. "I'm sorry, Mr. Petrillo. But we have no applications for building permits or a change in zoning for that address. When did Dr. Gutierrez say he filed those forms?"

"I don't know. Must have been a few weeks ago. He ain't here right now. I'm gonna have him call you back. First, I'm gonna yank my crew offa this and see if we can earn some money today." I hung up.

I made a list of the facts I'd learned this morning and tried to assemble them into a pattern that made sense. No matter how I arranged them, two seemingly contradictory conclusions remained. When I tried to marry them off, I had to explain why Dr. Rolando Gutierrez had elected to expose himself to so much risk if anything went wrong in his practice just to avoid leaving a paper trail.

I was just about out of frayed ends to play with. The chances of tracking Gutierrez through Argentine records were infinitesimal. I could swing by his place, take a couple of photos of him, run them by the hotel staff and see if I could get a positive I.D. That would help Whitney the most.

The first thing I needed to know was Gutierrez's work schedule. I called the mental health center and found out that he worked only ten hours a week at the center and always at night. That meant he'd be home days, trying to pay off that mortgage. A Georgetown address doesn't come cheaply.

There was one more thing I could do before this case fizzled out like a wet firecracker. I called an old lacrosse buddy of mine who was now chief surgeon at a shock trauma unit in Baltimore.

"Traumatology. Dr. Marks's office."

"Elliot Marks please."

"Senior or junior?"

"Junior."

"Hold on."

"Elliot Marks, Jr."

"How's it going, Elliot."

"Leo, how are you? Long time no see."

"Fine, Elliot. I've got a question for you. You started out in psychiatry, didn't you?"

"Yeah, but that can't be the question."

"No, it's not. I've got a guy with a less than therapeutic dose of Meprobamotrin in him, and some alcohol—"

"You've got a dead guy."

"I know. I've been told that the interaction effect is lethal and you need very little of the drug to trigger it."

"That's correct."

"But there's one more thing. I don't think he wanted to kill himself. I think he wanted to get off the medication. Why would he do something as dangerous as drink on that medication?"

"Was he warned about the consequences?"

"Yeah, I'm pretty sure he was."

"Let me think about this for a minute." The minute dragged on.

"There's one way it could happen. Do you know what a rebound effect is?"

"No."

"If your guy were to stop taking the medication abruptly, not taper off, there would be a rebound effect."

"Which is?"

"Whatever his original symptoms were would flare up again to an exacerbated degree. He'd probably experience a rush of anxiety, muscle twitches, tremors, possibly vomiting and ataxia, even delirium and hallucinations."

"So if he was feeling that bad he might start drinking to calm himself down, or he might be so confused he wouldn't remember not to drink?"

"Sure. He'd wind up permanently calm though."

"How long does this reaction last?"

"The onset can be anywhere from twelve to forty-eight hours after terminating the medication, and it passes in about the same amount of time."

"What if someone told this guy to take a drink to calm down?"

"They might just as well have given him a death sentence."

"Thanks, Elliot. What do you say we catch the Hopkins-Maryland game in the spring?"

"Love to. Don't be such a stranger."

"I won't. And thanks."

If you were the executioner, Dr. Gutierrez, what was Malcolm Donnelly's crime?

Chapter 27

I LOOKED OVER MY NOTES. Did Gutierrez and Donnelly know each other in Argentina? Gutierrez's practice: very low profile and very high risk. He had to be pretty sure than nothing could go wrong or that there was no way to report it. I was very curious about the good doctor's practice and time was of the essence. Nate would move quickly to get access to Donnelly's records and start litigation. That would drive everyone to ground. This might well be my one chance to catch Gutierrez off guard. I had the feeling that forewarned he'd be invincible.

In the bedroom, I threw my surveillance gear into a small duffel bag. On the way out to the car, I remembered that I had to stop at Dr. Skrepinski's office to get my stitches taken out. He was not glad to see me when I walked into his office, but he brightened when it was clear that I wasn't appearing in Odorama. When he was done, I looked at my face and had to give the man credit. The suture line was damn near invisible. Unshaven, I could see that it would appear in relief if I tried to grow a beard.

After a short stop to pick up lunch, I pulled past Gutierrez's house and parked in an alleyway that gave me a good vantage point. I took my binoculars, camera, windbreaker, hat, sunglasses and books out of my bag and spread them on the seat next to me.

As I was finishing off an essay by Allen Wheelis, Gutierrez came into view. He was accompanied by a sandy-haired boy. The boy was slight, and wore baggy olive drab pants and a black shirt. He preceded Gutierrez down the stairs to the street and stood with his head down and his hands shoved deep into his pockets. His hair was cut short and butch-waxed to stand straight up.

A car came around the corner and pulled up in front of the house. The driver looked strangely familiar to me. I couldn't place the face exactly but I knew I had seen it before. Gutierrez and the boy climbed into the car and it pulled away. I jotted down the tag numbers on my notepad and followed them. They were diplomatic plates.

Twenty minutes later the car parked and Gutierrez and the boy got out. They walked across Constitution Avenue to the Vietnam Veterans Memorial. In the car I slipped on my jacket, hat and sunglasses, hung the binoculars and camera around my neck and got out to follow them. Ahead of me, Gutierrez and the boy walked at a leisurely pace. The boy spoke animatedly to Gutierrez. At times he seemed quite agitated as if he were pleading with him, perhaps. Gutierrez smiled often at the boy and made palms-down motions for him to calm down or slow down.

We walked by the cordoned-off areas around the blasted wall. Repair crews were removing the ruined panels so that they could be replaced. The one where Arnie had picked up little James Tucker Calhoun and held him out to touch his namesake was already gone. Gutierrez stopped with the boy and pointed at the wall and at the spot on the knoll where the bomb had gone off. After a heated discussion the two of them walked back and got into the car. I barely made it to my car in time to follow them up Constitution Avenue.

Fortunately, they weren't going very far. When they stopped, Gutierrez sent the boy across the street to wait for him. While he stood and spoke to the driver I was able to get three good shots of him. I took one of the driver for good measure. Maybe it would help me recall where I had seen him before. Gutierrez crossed over to join the boy and they entered a large, impressive marble building.

Following them in, I looked up and saw that it was the headquarters of the InterAmerican Federation. Inside, I saw Gutierrez standing across a courtyard from me. He was in a great hall, continuing his show-and-tell session with the boy. I turned away from them and looked at the security officer at the front desk. His badge indicated he was from one of the larger private security firms in town. I looked around and counted three security officers, all unarmed. Behind the desk were three television monitors. The seated guard was watching them. One of the other guards greeted people as they entered the building and the third one did slow laps around the floor.

Gutierrez was coming back towards me. As he approached, I reached down and picked up a pamphlet on the federation's history and function. I was reading that the building and all its grounds were international property ceded by the United States to all the countries of the region when Gutierrez passed by and went into the bathroom with the boy. I flipped through the pamphlet to the map of the building and its grounds in the back and watched for Gutierrez to emerge.

I was curious about what was so interesting to Gutierrez about the great hall so I walked back to it and checked it out. All the time I was careful to keep an eye on the bathroom door.

It was a magnificent room. The floor was herringbone parquet. One wall had floor-to-ceiling stained glass windows depicting the tortuous path of progress in the region. To look at it, Jesus had had more fun at the stations of the cross. The other two walls were mirrored. Enormous chandeliers hung from the ceiling. When lit, the effect with those mirrored walls would be dazzling. The vaulted ceilings had to be thirty feet high, and there was more ornate scrollwork on the walls than on an heiress's wedding cake.

The strolling guard approached me. "Excuse me, what do they use this room for?" I asked.

"Formal state functions, receptions for visiting heads of state, treaty signing, that sort of thing."

"Oh. Who's in charge of security when the building is in use?"

"The security forces of whatever nation is hosting the

function take charge of the building. We're here to assist and observe the public when the building is not in use. It's open at no charge to anyone who wants to visit."

"I see. Thank you." I didn't have any more time for chitchat. Gutierrez and the boy were leaving. I hurried out after them.

The car that brought them there was waiting when they emerged. At the curb Gutierrez spoke to the boy. First he waved an admonishing finger at the boy, who averted his eyes. Finally he patted the boy's cheek and he brightened up. I would have to pass right by them to get to my car. I decided to stop the tail rather than blow my cover. Gutierrez climbed into the car and the driver gunned the motor. The BMW sped across the intersection against the light.

I stood there wondering what I had been watching. An unorthodox treatment program, maybe? Current events as psychotherapy for the ambulatory schizophrenic? What I was watching was the boy himself, now striding away up the street. I rolled the pamphlet up, stuck it in my back pocket, and followed the boy past "The Place Where Ronnie Dwells." At Farragut West we caught the Metro.

I stood on the platform watching the boy whistling a tune to himself. In a couple of minutes, the lights set into the floor began to flash, announcing the train's arrival. We climbed aboard the same car and rode the metal earthworm into the darkness. The orange line took us over to Foggy Bottom where we rode the elevator up to the street level. The boy walked briskly up Twenty-third Street towards M Street. An invigorating fifteen minutes later we were back in Georgetown.

I settled into a comfortable walk behind the boy. He trudged on, his hands jammed deep into his baggy pants, his shoulders hunched against an imaginary wind. We wandered through the commercial center of Georgetown. The sidewalks became more crowded. I slalomed along behind the boy. He walked with his head down, forcing everyone to walk around him to avoid a collision. As we approached the Wisconsin Avenue intersection, I saw a very attractive woman walking towards us. Her tight jeans were tucked into soft leather boots. A ribbed turtleneck of forest green and a designer knapsack purse slung over her right shoulder completed the look. Just in from Middleburg to pick up her jodhpurs, then out again. Her chestnut hair was pulled back into a sleek ponytail. The boy walked on, blind to her charms. As she passed, his head swivelled and he leered at her. The exorcist couldn't be far behind.

At Wisconsin Avenue, he stopped for a moment, watched the traffic and stepped off the curb. Good luck, kid. A ghost would have trouble crossing here against the light. I stood next to him and stared resolutely ahead. He never looked at me. We crossed the intersection and I let him stretch out a reasonable lead on me. Abruptly, he turned into a store entrance. I hurried to catch up with him.

As I entered the store, I looked up and read the sign: The Eye of the Storm: Interdimensional Portal & Bookstore. I whistled the *Twilight Zone* theme as I entered parts unknown. The left wall of the front room was floor to ceiling books. In the center was a long table covered with boxes into which were stuffed plastic wrapped comic books at astronomical prices. The first issue of anything was worth hundreds of dollars. Two rotating wire racks of more current artifacts anchored this table to the time-space continuum. A group of kids were poring over them like archeologists. "Wow, look at this," I heard. "*Deathblast* number one, incredible, I gotta have this." I'd bet that the Shroud of Turin didn't get such a welcome.

Huge color portraits of superheroes were everywhere. They were all engaged in battle with some misshapen villain. It was clear that evil was not good for your complexion. Most of these heroes fired some sort of powerblast from their hands, eyes or any other handy limb or orifice. Perhaps this was rooted in an adolescent fear of new and strange body products. The female superheroes all looked like they were out of *Playboy* by *Guns and Ammo*. Next we'll have *Bimbo of Fortune* magazine.

I looked around for the boy. He was leaning against the wall, reading a comic. I picked one up and skimmed it. Apparently the fate of the universe was in the hands of a guy who couldn't get a date on Friday night. Of course, under stress, his mutated hormones kicked in and with life as we know it hanging in the balance, this guy could move planets, warp time and kick a few butts. If only I'd known that, I'd have scanned the skies more often on Friday nights. When asked "Watcha doin' tonight? Wanna go to a party?" "Naw, I've got a universe to save. I'll take a raincheck" could have been my reply.

The behemoth behind the counter bellowed at a browser, "Five-minute reading limit. If you ain't gonna buy it, put it back." I looked over at crater face. If the aesthetics of this place held true then he was evil. He was big and sloppy with an enormous beer gut hanging over his belt. The T-shirt he wore read, 'If you see this body being operated in an unsafe manner, mind your own f-ing business.' His beard was long and unkempt, as was his ponytail. He sat leaning back against the wall, looking like he'd been thrown against it and was sliding to the floor. Only the chair beneath him halted his progress. His body had the tensile strength of ice cream in August.

The boy picked up a few comics and moved on. I scanned the wall of science fiction novels and looked fondly at the jackets of some of my favorites: Blish, Budrys, Haldeman, Robinson, Sturgeon. A book entitled *Neuromancer* had apparently won every award imaginable. I picked up a copy and followed the boy to an alcove in the back of the store. This area was devoted to role-playing games. The boy fingered books of spells and die-cast images of power. Assembly line voodoo.

At the counter the boy set down the comics he wanted. I was next to him in line. An alabaster-skinned girl with a wild mane of Day-Glo yellow hair and stone-encrusted crucifix earrings rang up the sale. I blanched. The comics must have been ten bucks each. The boy reached into his pants and came out with some scrunched-up bills. After smoothing them out, he was still three bucks short.

"Hey, how about you put it on my tab, Gino?" he said to the big man.

"Hey, how about you carry enough money on you, Marty?"

"Jesus, you know I'm good for it."

"Yeah, but I'm sick and tired of having to chase after you for the money, Marty. We're squared away, let's leave it like that."

"Jesus Christ, Gino. Give me a break."

The girl behind the counter picked up her cigarette, took a drag, rolled her eyes up and sighed.

"No, you give me a break, Marty. Put something back or just leave the store. I've got a business to run here and I've got a line behind you already." The blob slid off the stool, hooked his thumbs under his belt and hoisted his jeans over his gut. I guessed it was supposed to be a menacing gesture, one that showed single-mindedness and sincerity of purpose. The immediate retreat of the jeans from their high-water mark undid all that. I smiled but didn't laugh.

"How much short is he?" I asked.

"Three-forty," the cashier said. Staring hard at me, she blew a smoke ring out of her mouth. Her black T-shirt read 'I Am the Class of '69.'

"Here, tack it onto this." I handed her the book. She rang up both of the sales.

Marty scooped up his comics and said, "Thanks, man, I really appreciate that. Things like this disappear if you don't get 'em right away. And," he said looking pointedly at the fat man, "I'm good for it."

"No sweat."

She gave me back my change and said, "You want a bag for that?"

"No, thanks. I don't need one."

"Whatever." She smirked. She took another drag on her cigarette and slowly let out a whole chain of smokey *O*'s that drifted over Marty's head. I was impressed. I picked up my book and turned to leave. Marty was already gone. On the way out I saw the girl's image in the front window. She was still blowing smoke.

Chapter 28

MARTY WAS WAITING for me outside the store. Leaning up against the wall, he was immersed in his comic book. He looked up as I stepped down beside him.

"Thanks a lot, man, really, I appreciate it." His brow furrowed and he turned his face slightly away from me. "How come you did that? I don't know you."

"You're wondering if I'm trying to pick you up, right?" I assumed the lean right next to him.

"The thought had crossed my mind," he said.

"But you let me do it anyway?"

"Yeah, 'cause I wanted the comics. But let me tell you, if you put a hand on me, I'll tell Gino and he hates fags worse than anything. He'd come out here and squash you."

I had a middling urge to wipe the smirk off his face with the sidewalk. "Well, relax. You're not my type."

"You like Mona, huh?"

"She the girl behind the counter?"

"Yeah, she's a real man-eater, know what I mean?" He leered, the same way he had at the girl he'd passed on the street.

"You don't say."

"I do."

"Is this firsthand knowledge or just gossip?"

"Well . . ."

"Why don't I go ask Mona if she remembers you." I started to push off from the wall.

"All right, all right. I haven't had her myself, actually. Just, you know, heard things."

I leaned back up against the wall. "To answer your question, I did it because I remember what it's like to want something real bad and come up a dollar short and a day late. Hell, a valuable comic like that isn't gonna sit around in his stacks very long. Secondly, Gino said you were good for it and he doesn't look like one of the Little Sisters of the Poor to me."

"No sweat, man. I don't live too far from here. I can get you the money."

"Okay, let's go."

"No. Wait. I've got an idea." He'd started bouncing around on the balls of his feet, like an adrenaline-crazed bantamweight.

"And that idea is?"

"I've got a couple of passes for the movie up the street. They're showing *The Obliterator*. Have you seen it?"

"No. I haven't."

"Want to go? My treat. A ticket's at least three-fifty, what do you say? Besides, it's better to see it with somebody."

"Sure. Let's go." So much for getting a look at his digs. Missing *The Obliterator* had not been an oversight on my cultural calendar. One more in the seemingly endless series of '-ator' movies. We were probably condemned to endure yet the Incinerator, the Vaccinator, the Castigator, all the way down to the most loathsome of modern villains: the Administrator. Then there'd be a go-round of sequels, prequels, and spin-offs until not a man, woman or child in this country had been spared.

"You'll really like it. You won't believe how many people get killed in this. It's incredible, and the Obliterator, he's absolutely awesome. You'll love it." I had no idea why he was so sure of this.

"By the way, my name's Sam. Samuel T. Miller to be exact, but Sam's fine." I stuck out my hand. He shook it.

"Martin. Martin Gregorio Fernandez. Marty is fine."

"Pleased to meet you," I said.

"Likewise."

Two blocks later I found myself in line with Marty and

another twenty of the Obliterator's fans. Most of them were young men, eighteen to twenty-two. Celluloid omnivores with cast-iron guts and no taste buds. There were a couple of older guys in suits, here for a fantasy fix before they put a lid on the id. Marty gave in the passes and we went down to the seats. He wanted to sit right under the screen. I got him to compromise at row twelve. Everyone else had spread out throughout the theatre.

Marty leaned over to me and whispered, "Do you smoke?"
I said, "No."
"I've got a couple of joints. Beautiful stuff. You sure you don't want any?"
"No, thanks. That's okay."
"No problem. The stuff really mellows me out. I take a couple of hits before the movie starts. It makes it all better. You know, the blood is brighter and everything. And it looks like it's moving real slow when it comes out. The grass keeps me from getting uptight about it."

Wonderful. I'm spending an afternoon in a butcher shop with one of the living dead for a guide. "You smoke often?" I asked, intrigued at how easily he talked about himself to a stranger.

"Nah, not anymore. I used to smoke all the time. I was uptight all the time. But my shrink taught me self-hypnosis. Now I can turn myself off any time I want to."

"Why not do that here, then?"

" 'Cause sometimes I still like the feeling that grass gives me. Like here it makes the movie more real and less real. Like it's brighter, larger, more of everything. But you don't really think about what you're seeing. It's just like seeing it more or better. I don't know. I just do it sometimes."

"Was it hard to learn to hypnotize yourself?"

"No, not really. My doctor said I'm real good at it. I guess I've been able to do it all along, only I just didn't know what it was. I just used to space out—in school, everywhere. Used to drive my old man crazy. He'd be talking to me and I'd be somewhere else. Then I'd come back and ask him, 'What did you say?' He'd go batshit."

"I can imagine. So this is something you think you were just born with?"

"Yeah, I guess so. I've always been able to do it. I was always daydreaming. I started to do it more after Ralph died, though."

"Who's Ralph?"

"Oh, Ralph was my brother."

"When did he die?"

"Long time ago."

"How did it happen?"

"He caught a mortar shell in his foxhole. Blew him all to hell." Marty pulled out his joint and lit it.

"How old were you when it happened?"

"Me, oh, I guess I was six. Ralph was going to be twenty that fall."

"I'm sorry, Marty. You must miss him very much." Marty took another long drag. I looked around and saw that he wasn't the only one preparing for the Obliterator's arrival.

"Yeah, I guess so. Mostly I feel like his death really fucked up my life."

"How so?"

"When Ralph died, my father really lost it. He felt responsible because he was part of the government that sent Ralph over there."

"Oh, what did your father do?"

"Back then he was in the Office for Hispanic Affairs. After that he got a promotion, I guess, into the embassy staff down in Honduras for a while. Nothing really helped. He never got over Ralph's death. He felt that the government had abandoned the guys they sent over there and he just stopped believing in the government. So he retired. Now he just sits around the house and watches T.V. When I turned eighteen I'd had it. I just had to get out. He was driving me crazy. Nothing I could do was good enough. I mean, I didn't kill Ralph, did I? I just had to split."

"When was this?"

"Oh, last summer, maybe six months ago. Right before I got into therapy."

"So, has it helped?"

"Yeah, yeah . . ." He waved me off and took another hit. "Movie's gonna start. Hold on to your seat."

"Right." I wanted to induce a trance state in myself. In it, Samantha and I would be on a Caribbean island. We would have a beach all to ourselves. Just us and the rum and mangoes and snorkels and no clothes. It just wouldn't come to me. Instead I got ninety minutes of high-tech mayhem. Spurting torsos, exploding cars and shattering glass were presented with an irritating voice-over monologue about the lonely quest of the Obliterator. As far as I could tell, the movie ended because they'd blown up every prop and killed every extra in California. A trailer promised that we hadn't seen the end of the Obliterator. Oh, joy!

The lights came on. Marty shook his head. "Wow. Incredible. Just awesome."

"I'll say."

We filed out of the theatre. On the sidewalk we shook hands.

"Thanks for the movie. I enjoyed talking with you," I said.

"You gotta go?" This kid had kicked puppy written all over him.

"Well, I don't have to. I just figured we were square. You know." I started to turn away. I was playing the kid's hunger for all it was worth. I turned back and said, "There is something I wanted to ask you about."

"Sure. Great. Hey, whatever." He brightened up immediately.

"Let's find a pizza place. That okay?"

"Sure."

A half block down on M Street we found one. I ordered a large pizza with mushrooms and sausage, and two beers. We took the beers back to a table. The pizza would take fifteen minutes, they said. At the table, I sipped my beer.

"What I wanted to talk to you about is your therapist."

Marty put his beer down and looked at me warily.

"No, no. I don't want to talk to you about your therapy.

I know that's very personal, private stuff. It's just that I'd been thinking of getting into therapy myself. I just seem to be having problems with the women I'm meeting these days. I wonder if you think this guy is any good. Whether he could help me? Or if he even had time to see anyone new. I mean, shrinks in this town are real busy."

"Oh, Dr. G is great. He's really helped me a lot."

"How did you find him? The Yellow Pages?"

"Naw. I had to go get an evaluation from a psychiatrist. It was a condition of my vocational rehab. program. I'd bagged school, see, and I didn't have a job, and my old man was ready to toss my ass out of the house. So I went to voc. rehab. to see about getting some job training and placement. They said I had to go down and see a shrink. Shit, what a drag, but it was that or hit the streets, so I went. Anyway, I saw this guy Dr. Bronstein or something. He was a real jerk. Anyway, next thing I hear, a couple of days later Dr. G. gives me a call. He tells me that he's part of a research program that N.I.H. or someone is running. He'll see me for free. He even got D.V.R. to put me up in an apartment of my own. An independent living program, I think he called it."

"That's fascinating. Can you tell me what the research is?"

"I'm not real sure. He said that part of the study would be ruined if you knew what the purpose was. But I'll be told at the end of the study. He showed me a folder full of graphs and gobbledygook. Something about 'Self-Control and Hypnosis in Young Adults.'"

"How long has the study been going on?"

"I've been seeing Dr. G. for about six months now."

"How often do you go to see him?"

"Three times a week at first. Now twice a week."

"Do you know how many subjects there are in the study?"

"No. Dr. G. has told me that I've shown the best response in teaching myself hypnosis. We're all supposed to get together at the end to be debriefed, you know."

"So Dr. G. is a good guy. Pretty easy to talk to, is he?"

"Oh yeah. He's real laid back. You feel like you could tell him anything. Sometimes it's like you want to tell him everything. You know what I mean?"

"Yeah. I know what you mean." Do I ever. "Okay. You've sold me on him. Where is his office? Is it nearby?"

"Yeah. His office is over on 38th Street. It's in the basement of his house."

"This hypnosis stuff, I mean, is it like you see on television? You know, spinning watches and making people bark like dogs?"

"No. No. It's nothing like that. I thought it was like that too when I first went. But it's real different. He calls that stuff stage hypnosis. That's for cheap tricks, he says. This is clinical hypnosis, he calls it."

"I have to admit, it'd be a little scary letting somebody take over your mind like that. You'd have to really trust him." I shook my head in doubt.

"No, it's not like that. It's not like somebody taking over your mind. It's like you want to give up control, and so if somebody else has it for a while that's okay because you gave it to them. You could take it back if you wanted to. You just don't want to. That's all."

"Like I said, you must really trust this guy."

"Yeah, I guess I do. He's done more for me in the last six months than the whole rest of my life combined. I really owe him a lot."

"Can I use your name when I call, you know, tell him who referred me?"

"Sure. No problem. I'll tell him to expect a call from you when I see him tomorrow."

"Oh, does he usually have weekend hours? That would be real convenient for me."

"No. This is the first time. He says I'm on the verge of a breakthrough. Something really big and important, so he wants to see me tomorrow. We had a session today. It was very intense, very intense."

"Well, I hope it goes well for you."

Our pizza arrived and we went at it like piranhas at a

picnic. Less than ten minutes later there wasn't much more than a splotch of tomato sauce to identify what had been there. I wiped my mouth, finished my beer and pushed my chair back. Marty looked up.

"You gotta go?" he asked.

"Yeah, I gotta go. One of those women I've been having trouble with." I shrugged my shoulders and held my hands out, palms up. Unspoken, we shared the age-old lament, What's a guy to do? You can't live with 'em, you can't live without 'em. Marty and I shook hands and I left the pizza parlor.

I hiked up M Street and across the Francis Scott Key Bridge into Arlington. In 1847 the land that is now Arlington County retroceded from the Federal District back to Virginia. One reason for the move was Southern displeasure with federal control of the port city of Alexandria. This was a tiny harbinger of the rift that the Potomac would demarcate only fourteen years later. These days, Arlington and Fairfax counties and Alexandria are the bedroom communities for that same federal government. Richmond views this area as a fat federal tumor that has erupted in their midst and one that isn't very Southern or very Virginian at all.

I caught the orange line subway in Rosslyn and rode back under the river to Farragut West. From there I walked back to my car. Thirty minutes later I pulled up to my house. Inside, I emptied out my duffel bag. There were no messages with my answering service. I called Arnie and got no answer. Then I called Josh Walters and promised him that I'd be bringing by some work first thing tomorrow.

Sitting in my recliner I took a couple of laps around the "vast wasteland," now cable-enhanced to almost a hundred varieties of white noise. I turned the set off and stuck the Swimming Pool Q's into the cassette player. Anne Richmond Boston's voice, as supple and sinuous as a python, coiled itself around and over the guitar lines as she sang "I don't think there'll be a new road through." Getting the news from her almost broke my heart. I sat for a while and tried to imagine what was going to come pouring out through the breakthrough in Marty Fernandez's mind. I fell asleep in that chair with the question still unanswered. For a change, I slept through whatever dreams I had.

Chapter 29

WHEN I AWOKE, I was still in the same chair. A long hot shower helped get the kinks out. I shaved for the first time in a few days, and did so very carefully. The newspaper was running the bomber photo on page two. Page one had the first droolings from the Hand of Allah group. I skimmed the paper as I set up the coffee and scrambled a couple of eggs. When I'd eaten I called Arnie. There was still no answer.

I repacked my duffel for today's surveillance and got ready to sit on Dr. Gutierrez. This would probably be the end of the road for this case. On Monday, Nate would be down at the center with Marta, requesting access to her husband's file. Maybe the photos would jog a memory at the hotel. Maybe a typewriter match could be made with the one in his office. If those came through maybe I could force Nate or the police to do the kind of background check that might put Gutierrez and Donnelly cheek by jowl and yield a plausible motive. Even with all those things, the M.O. for this one was a pip. Donnelly was dead because Gutierrez had played on and amplified his vulnerability and confusion and got him to kill himself.

I stopped for a moment and wondered why I was bothering to pursue this. For starters, I felt I owed it to Truman Whitney. I had put him and his career on the hook. The least I could do was run down every possibility of getting him off. But there was another reason. Gutierrez had whipped me. We had crossed wills in that soundproofed room of his and he had won. He had chased me into a corner and I had run for my life at the end. I wanted another shot at him. I'm a terrible loser. And I had this feeling that Marty Fernandez's breakthrough wouldn't bring him any peace at all.

I called Samantha and got her answering machine. I told it to say hello to sleepy head, that I hoped she'd had a nice time with Sandra and that I'd call her later. I dropped the film with Josh and told him that I'd pick up the cropped enlargements later this evening.

I had lunch at Las Pampas, which for my money, is the best steakhouse in town. With someone else's money I might give Morton's the nod.

From there it took me twenty minutes of circling the block to find a parking spot with a good view of the front and side of Gutierrez's house. Once I had set up shop behind the Camaro's smoked glass, the first thing to do was make sure that Gutierrez was home. I stuffed my cheeks with a handkerchief and dialed his number. The cellular car phone is the greatest boon to surveillance since the widemouthed mason jar.

"Hello," he said.

I pinched my nostrils shut and said, "Ith Doloreth there?"

"I'm sorry, you have the wrong number."

"Thorry." I hung up.

So Rolando was home. There was nothing to do but wait. It was one slow day in Georgetown. No one had come to his house by noon, and he hadn't gone anywhere. I worked diligently at a crossword pun-zle. By three I had solved only three items. A church pamphlet on the dangers of masturbation was "Onan the destroyer"; the Greek demolition firm that blew itself up was "Edifice Wrecks"; and the review of the book *Hitler Never Died* was "Sure to raise a furor." Marty Fernandez was a no-show so far. I decided to try to force things a little bit.

What I really wanted was a typing sample from Gutierrez's machine. If he saw me for a second session he'd have to bill me and I could ask for a statement. I called Gutierrez again.

"Hello, Dr. Gutierrez. This is Francis Jerome. I was

wondering if I could see you again. That session we had really unhinged me. Could I see you today maybe?"

"I'm sorry, Mr. Jerome. I do not have weekend office hours. Perhaps something early next week. Would that be all right?"

"I don't know. I've been having some really weird dreams since we talked. Even when I'm awake I feel like I'm in a dream. You know what I mean? I mean, I'm worrying that I'm going crazy."

"This sometimes occurs when there has been a breakthrough of long-repressed material. It can be quite uncomfortable, but I assure you, Mr. Jerome, you are not going crazy. Our first session showed that your defenses are functioning very well. If you feel it's an emergency, I suggest you admit yourself to the local hospital emergency room for observation."

"I don't know. I don't even trust myself to drive, the way I'm feeling right now."

"All right. I'll tell you what. I have a meeting to attend at four-thirty. I'll be back at five o'clock. Call me here at that time. If you aren't feeling any better I'll send a cab over to pick you up and I'll meet you at the hospital."

"Thanks, Dr. Gutierrez. I really wouldn't feel comfortable talking to anyone else but you."

"I understand, Mr. Jerome. Call here at five."

I settled back into waiting. I wasn't doing very well with the pun-zle, so I picked up the brochure I'd taken from the federation building yesterday. I flipped through the history and statement of purpose sections and unfolded the map in the back. After orienting myself, I tried to visualize the great hall, the formal gardens, and the other rooms I had seen. Each country's office was identified by its flag. There was a dotted line connecting the main building to the new library. I couldn't remember seeing a path or walkway when I'd looked out the back windows of the great hall. Maybe it was just "proposed." I folded up the map and slipped it inside my jacket pocket.

As four-thirty approached, I made up my mind to use the opportunity to get a typing sample and maybe a peek at the files, if there were any, on Malcolm Donnelly and Marty Fernandez.

I called Samantha. "Hello." she said.

"Samantha, I've made another appointment with Gutierrez. I don't expect any trouble, but just in case, if you don't hear from me by five o'clock, call the police. Tell them anything to get them over here. Okay?"

"Where are you?"

I gave her the address. "Thanks."

"Do you have to do this? Why not let the cops do it? That's their job."

"There's nothing for them to do. That is, unless I don't come out at five o'clock. I'm at the end of this one. This is the last straw to grasp at. If it doesn't pan out, I'll put it to rest. We can take those few days off you wanted to."

"Leo, be careful. That last straw is the one that broke the camel's back."

I had the feeling she was talking about herself. "I will. Remember, if I don't call you at five o'clock sharp, call the cavalry, pronto."

"Will do."

As I put the phone down, the same BMW I'd seen yesterday pulled up. Gutierrez appeared, walked over to the car and climbed in. When it had gone around the corner, I got out of my car, stretched out my kinks and sauntered across the street. I patted my pockets to make sure that I had everything I needed. At the back door, I took out my set of picks, selected one and slipped it in as delicately as I had with my first girlfriend when we were but sixteen. This lock gave way as easily as she had. I put the pick back in my case, turned the knob and walked in.

I hurried down to Gutierrez's office and found it unlocked. I walked over to the desk and flipped on the table lamp. There were some charts on the desk. The top one was for Martin Gregorio Fernandez. I flipped it open. The first page was covered with notes from the therapy sessions. The last note had today's date. I read it first.

11/16/86 Martin very disturbed today, quite agitated. Anger at father mounting. Feels he cannot do anything to impress him, to validate his sense of self-worth. Feels inferior to brother Ralph, who he thinks died a hero, and is seen as such by father. Fantasies of violence abound. I am concerned about breakdown of repression barrier and psychotic decompensation. No explicit threats or plans mentioned. Denies that he has access to any weapons. Has agreed to phone check-in if he feels he is losing control.

I read all the previous entries. There was an orderly progression of mounting concern about the sanity and self-control of one Martin G. Fernandez. A variety of precautionary actions taken by Dr. Gutierrez were carefully documented. It was a model of medical record keeping. Only one thing was missing. There wasn't a single federal research form in the chart. No statement of patients' rights, no informed consent form, nothing. If you're going to spend Uncle Sam's money, there's one thing you can count on: you're going to have to document everything. The toilet paper the government uses is three ply. Two for permission to wipe your ass and one to do it with. There was nothing like that here. No, this chart was all fiction.

I closed the file and slid it aside to see who else's records were out. Perhaps it was another of the good doctor's "subjects." I read the name on the file. It was the case record for one Samuel T. Miller.

I stared at the file and blinked my eyes, but the title didn't change. It was definitely time to leave. My neck hairs prickled with an animal awareness of the hunter's gaze. One instant you're quiet and small, invisible. The next second, you're frozen, stark naked in a cold hard glare. It was getting hard to swallow. The light flipping on didn't help.

Chapter 30

"Good evening, Mr. Miller."

I turned slowly, already certain of what I'd see. Gutierrez was in the doorway with a pistol in his hand and a big, ugly dog on a short lead. Marty Fernandez stood next to him, grinning idiotically. The driver of the BMW appeared behind them. I finally realized where I'd seen him before. We'd had breakfast together the last two days. He'd been on page one of *The Post*.

"Martin," Gutierrez said, "you've done us a great service by exposing this enemy of our cause. Go upstairs now. I'll be up in a minute."

When Marty had gone, Gutierrez spoke to the other man. "Search him, Jesus." Jesus crossed to me, never once getting into Gutierrez's line of fire, and expertly patted me down. Good-bye lock picks, microrecorder, and Colt .45. Jesus showed Gutierrez his loot. The doctor said, "Go upstairs with Martin. I'll call you if I need you."

Gutierrez looked at me and shook his head. "What are we to do with you, Mr. Miller? Or is it Mr. Jerome? Or something else altogether?" He chuckled. "I need to know what you know, Mr. Miller, and I need to know it quickly. We've invested too much and come too far to be thwarted now."

"Hey, no sweat, man. I'll tell you whatever you want to know. Let's deal. I mean, I ain't sticking my neck out for anybody." I flicked a look at Gutierrez's clock. If I could keep flapping my gums for fifteen minutes or so the boys in blue would be here.

"I'm sorry, Mr. Miller. My experience tells me not to trust people who tell their secrets too easily. I trust what I can buy with blood. I don't have time to take you apart right now and I won't move until I know what you know. You've created a number of problems for me."

I decided to start singing before he decided that a .38 in the head was the best solution to his problems. Maybe I could buy some time by keeping my story very hazy and letting him fill in the details.

I let fly with a high, hard one. "We know about your plans for the boy."

"Oh, you do. Then why are you in here rifling my records? No, I think not. You may suspect but you do not know."

He hit that one out of the park. I threw him a change up. "How'd you kill him?"

"Kill who?" Gutierrez frowned.

"Malcolm Donnelly."

"Malcolm Donnelly? Are you really here because of Malcolm Donnelly? That wasn't simply a cover story?" Gutierrez shook his head in wonderment.

"I know you killed Donnelly and you've got something planned for that boy, something to do with the InterAmerican Federation."

"You've just solved a lot of my problems, Mr. Miller. If it's Malcolm Donnelly that you're concerned about, our discussion is over. This has nothing to do with him."

"Yeah, that may be true but you can't kill me. My partners know about everything."

"Mr. Miller, I doubt that. I'm not surprised that you tried that ploy. Believe me, I'm an expert on what people do under duress. But your first move you phrased as 'we know.' When that failed, you fell back to 'I know.' No, I think that there is no one else but you, Mr. Miller. And besides, there's no need to kill you."

"You can't let me walk out of here." Why was I so intent on digging my own grave?

"That's precisely what I intend to do, Mr. Miller. However, you won't walk out the same man who walked in."

"What's that supposed to mean?" Keep him talking.

"You did not read your file?"

"Sorry, I didn't get to it."

"Well, Mr. Miller, the file reveals that your paranoid delusions, memory losses and flattened affect were due to the frontal lobotomy that had been performed on you."

"You're kidding. You can't mean that."

"Oh, indeed I do, Mr. Miller." Gutierrez stepped closer. "A tranquilizer dart in the chest to sedate you. Curare perhaps. You'll feel everything but be unable to resist. A favorite of mine. Then I apply enough pressure with my thumbs to pop out your left eye, and then, while it hangs down on your cheek, a blade is inserted under the optic ridge into the bundle of nerve fibers that connect your brain's frontal lobes. Back and forth with the blade like a windshield wiper and you are erased, Mr. Miller. We'll pop your eye back in and from the outside you're the same man. But all you have been, all you have known, loved or remembered, will be lost to you. You'll be picked up wandering the streets. We'll drop you near a hospital. Not here in Washington, perhaps Baltimore or Richmond. They'll mistake you for a schizophrenic. Eventually, a halfway smart psychiatrist will put together your symptom picture and run a brain scan on you and figure out what has happened to you. You won't be able to tell them who your friends are because you won't remember them. I doubt that they'd think to look for you in the turnip bins of a mental hospital, especially of one in another city."

I thought to myself, that's not the way Arnie would go looking for me. It was little consolation, but if Gutierrez didn't get himself out of town, he was in for a rougher time than me. I peeked at the clock. I'd bought myself eight minutes. Seven to go. They say the truth will set you free. Time to give it a chance.

"If I'm no threat to you, then you can't have any fears about telling me what's going on here." I was hoping he would enjoy rubbing my face in his superiority. I wasn't wrong.

"True enough, Mr. Miller."

"Let's cut the crap then, I'm not Mr. Miller. My name is Leo Haggerty. And you are?"

"Colonel Bernardo Schmidt."

"Colonel? Aren't you even a doctor?"

"Oh, I am that too. I was in charge of the psychological torture unit of the Argentine secret police."

"So that's where Malcolm Donnelly knew you from."

"Yes. He recognized me at the clinic one day. He knew that I couldn't be in the United States legally. He threatened to expose me and have me deported back for trial if I didn't help him get custody of his children."

"Which you agreed to do."

"Of course. What a pathetic man. I told him to get off the medication he was on because it wouldn't look good in court."

"Which triggered a rebound effect."

"Very good, Mr. Haggerty. You've done your homework. I left a number for Malcolm to call day or night if his symptoms flared up. Of course they did. When he called me he was quite agitated and confused. I told him to take a drink or two to calm down and that I'd be right over. He was so desperate to stop the anxiety that he forgot that the combination was lethal."

"Death by suggestion. You brought the suicide note because you knew he'd be dead."

"Not exactly. I sent Jesus with the note and instructions on how to make Malcolm dead if he wasn't already dead when he got there. Very neat, don't you think?"

"Tidiness is next to godliness, I always say."

"Don't mock me, Mr. Haggerty. You will wish that your end was as swift and clean."

"Quite right. You are holding all the cards. My apologies."

There was a knock on the door. Gutierrez said, "*Sí?*"

Jesus stuck his head in the room. "There is someone at the front door. What do you want me to do about it?"

"Has Ernesto arrived yet?"

"Yes."

"Perhaps it is our 'observers.' I know what they look like.

I'll be right up to check on it." Gutierrez looked back at me. "Make yourself comfortable, Mr. Haggerty. Hansi here is a Pit Bull, a trained attack dog. Please understand that his instinctive ferocity has been tempered by diligent training. Unlike you or I, he has no doubts about what he is supposed to do. If you make any attempt to leave, Hansi will subdue you instantly. With a bite pressure of over a thousand pounds per square inch he can shatter your bones. If you are lucky you will pass out from the pain. You may yell all you want for help. The walls and ceiling are completely soundproofed. But then again, you already know that." He stroked the dog's neck and removed its collar. "Hansi, hold," he said. With that he smiled and left.

I smiled at the dog. It growled back. I knew the breed and this one was a giant, probably seventy pounds. They were bred for pit fighting and had the enormous jaws and chests of their cousins the bulldog but with enough leg under them to run down their victims.

We had a staring contest and Hansi with his black button eyes was the winner hands down. His breathing was a harsh panting sound and his retracted muzzle revealed a row of teeth that Bruce the Shark would have admired. Ever so slowly, I turned my head and looked at the clock. Five-o-three. The police should be here any minute.

The door opened. I looked up, smiling. It was Gutierrez. He stepped into the room and ordered the dog to sit. "Idiot. What is a grown man doing delivering pizzas for a living? And not even the right block."

I let out a slow exhalation of air. Hope exits with a bad smell on your breath. Would Samantha have forgotten to call? Was she lost in some reverie? I hoped her next book was a fucking best seller, but I probably wouldn't remember who she was to congratulate when I left here anyway.

"As long as we're having no secrets here, Colonel, how did you tumble on to me?" I was zero for two with this guy. Maybe I was out of my league.

"That was easy enough. I had placed a post-hypnotic

suggestion into Martin's unconscious that compels him to tell me if anyone questions him about our relationship. He called me late last night. The square patch on your face that he described matched the bandaged area that I had seen. When you called, as I expected you would, I baited you by telling you that I'd be out for a while. I went with Jesus to pick up Hansi in case we would need him and returned after you'd let yourself in."

"What are you going to do with the boy? He thinks you're the greatest thing since sliced bread."

"You might say I'm helping him become his heart's desire, or as your army slogan puts it, to 'be all you can be.' He wants to be a hero, like his brother. I am helping him achieve that dream." Gutierrez sat in his chair. His gun never wavered from the center of my chest.

"Doesn't sound like therapy to me."

"It isn't, although I doubt that Martin understands that, and I have been very helpful to him. He is no longer depressed or guilt-ridden. I've helped him free up all that energy for other uses."

"Such as?"

"Helping to prevent the meaningless deaths of Americans in Central America."

"What about the wall? I saw you with him at the wall."

"Really? So you had us under surveillance. What prompted you to do that? I thought that our session had gone very well. That I had convinced you of my simple desire to be of service."

"I had a dream."

"A dream, indeed. How did that lead you to suspect me?" Gutierrez cocked a quizzical eyebrow.

"At the end of the dream, you were trying to imprison me in my nightmare."

"Bravo, Mr. Haggerty. Very few people are willing to listen to their unconscious mind. Unfortunately, you lack the wisdom to heed its message. I will soon imprison you in your own nightmare."

"So what were you doing with him at the wall?"

"The purpose of that visit was to inflame him. To push him in the right direction."

"Which is?"

"The assassination of General Hortencio Villarosa this evening at the official party his government is throwing to celebrate tomorrow's signing of the treaty with the United States."

"You're sending this kid in there to kill Villarosa? Maybe I've missed something. Security is going to be tighter than on a blind date in Sicily."

"True but irrelevant."

I chewed on that one for a minute. "Let me guess—the head of security is in this with you?"

"Very good. He will receive a promotion after a decent interval. In recognition of his service to the coalition of generals and, shall we say, businessmen who feel that General Villarosa has been unwise in agreeing to allow the United States greater say in controlling the flow of a certain important crop in and out of his country in exchange for money and weapons to control the rebels."

"Christ, the cocaine dealers want him dead?"

"Of course. His country is a conduit for almost a billion dollars worth of business. They are not about to let him close that pipeline down because he thinks that American guns and money will protect him and ensure his remaining in power."

"So the cocaine dealers approached the generals with 'an offer they couldn't refuse'?"

"Exactly. They were agreeable. The cocaine dealers have enough money to assist in providing arms to the government. After all, a revolution would be bad for business. So the generals stay in power and the pipeline stays open. Everyone prospers. By having Villarosa killed by an American, suspicion is diverted away from the generals and there will be a breach in relations between the two countries. Temporary, of course, but enough to set treaty negotiations back to step one. It may be years before another crisis like this one hits the dealers. Your president will be out of office in less than two years. Who knows what your foreign policy will look like then?"

"If Marty thinks that you're for keeping the United States out of Central America and saving American lives, how do you think he'd react if he knew that it was you who blew up the wall?"

"How did you figure that out?"

"Jesus looks just like the pictures in the newspaper."

"Yes, well, he leaves the country tomorrow. The bombing was necessary to convince Martin of the seriousness of the situation. To fully recreate for him that emotional climate he felt when his brother was killed. To believe that American boys would die overseas, to believe that here was a chance to prevent what happened to his brother from happening again, to be a hero in his father's eyes and his own. Martin had to feel that there was a mandate for his actions, that he spoke for countless people who felt as he did. The bombing was, if you will, a special effect, something to give Martin's feelings the illusion of a reality outside of himself. We were running out of time and had to remove his remaining inhibitions. The people at the wall had to die, their blood had to be spilt so that Martin would feel desperate enough to act."

"So you're the Standing Committee on World Justice?"

"In a manner of speaking. It's what you would call a 'dummy corporation,' under which a variety of groups can conduct their business here."

"Such as certain Middle Eastern groups?"

"Yes. They very much like the idea of using Americans to kill Americans. Besides saving on their manpower, it confirms their belief that you are all corrupt and weak. There will be a couple of observers from The Hand of Allah there tonight. They will be watching the outcome of my work with Martin. They may wish to purchase my skills."

"And just what are those skills?"

"Personality reconstruction. All the tools have been around for quite a while: coercive hypnosis, psychosurgery and drugs. All that was required was careful study of their

application and a sufficient number of subjects to reach
scientifically precise conclusions."

"The 'disappeared ones'?"

"Yes. Torture for information is relatively simple work,
and torture for torture's sake is a bore, but to be able to
break down a personality and then reassemble it in any
way you choose is an enormous achievement."

"Don't flatter yourself. You may be able to break down
a poet, but you'll never be able to build one."

Gutierrez's slap rocked my head, my suture line was on
fire. "You don't know anything of what I can do."

"I do know that Marty's not a killer. He's a dreamer,
not a doer. And besides, I've always heard it said that hypnosis can't make you do something you wouldn't ordinarily
do."

"That's true as far as it goes. The trick is to make someone want to do something you want them to do. You say
that Martin is not a killer, but if you spent any time at
all with him you would know that he is obsessed with
fantasies of violence and heroism. All I have done is built
a bridge from his fantasies to my reality.

"I have buttressed his fantasies, not analyzed them.
Marty is now certain that he can recapture his father's love
by an act of violent heroism."

"Marty didn't sound like he gave a rat's ass for his old
man's love."

"That's all on the surface. Deep down he desperately
wants his father's love. He feels he lost it when his brother
died in Vietnam. I have simply let Marty know that I
believe Villarosa's death is necessary to avert another war,
and that such an act would save countless boys just like
his brother. Marty would be able to symbolically save his
brother."

"Why should Marty care what you think?"

"Because he trusts me. He thinks I care about him. He
doesn't want to disappoint me as he has his father. I am
merely using Marty's pathetic need for approval for my
own ends. He is exquisitely sensitive to the expectations
of others. It isn't even necessary to suggest that he kill

Villarosa. He is convinced that such an act will please both me and his father. It is Marty that is the loaded gun, not the revolver he will hold in his hand. The bombing at the wall cocked him, tonight at the party I need only point him in the right direction."

I shook my head. "You have an uncanny feel for the weaknesses of others. The kid never had a chance with you."

"Of course not. I hand-picked him. Once the cocaine consortium contacted me, they helped set me up here after I had to flee Argentina," Gutierrez explained. "It took a while to find the appropriate subject. Angry, isolated young men who hunger for the approval of a male authority figure are easy to find, but a Hispanic who had lost someone in Vietnam, that was harder."

"And your phonied-up records will present the picture of a lonely, sad, deranged boy losing his grip on reality and exploding in senseless violence. How will you explain his being with you at the party?"

"That won't be necessary. The chief of security will kill Martin right after General Villarosa falls. There will be a lengthy investigation afterwards. Those records confirm my relationship with Martin, but portray it in a different light, shall we say."

With that, Gutierrez rose and walked to the door. "Just relax, Mr. Haggerty. There's nothing you can do. Unless you'd like to try to get past Hansi. If you're lucky, he'll rip out your throat and save us both some inconvenience. Remember, the room is soundproofed, so we won't be able to hear your screams or be able to call him off." Gutierrez grinned, told the dog to "Hold" and backed out of my life.

Chapter 31

WELL, HANSI, I thought, it's you and me. I looked around the room for a weapon. What was I going to do, choke him on a medical record? There wasn't anything useful at all. I took a personal inventory: shoes, socks, shorts, pants, belt, shirt, empty holster, jacket. Nothing. I had no weapon and damn little time. I looked back at Hansi: faster than me, pound for pound stronger than me, bred and trained for one thing—to bring a man down in his tracks and keep him there. With my bare hands, I probably couldn't hurt him in any fashion. If I fed him my arm, how far would I get with a crushed forearm and a seventy-pound charm bracelet hanging from it? Not even to the door. If only Gutierrez hadn't taken his collar off. Maybe, just maybe, I could have strangled him with it. I looked down at my belt and then back at Hansi. He was just a rasping pant, flat eyes and all those damned teeth.

I slowly fed the end of the belt into my left palm and heard the soft click as the tongue popped out. Hansi growled and stiffened. Slowly, inch by inch I fed the belt from my right hand to my left and folded it back on itself into a tight loop. My hands never left my lap. I slipped one end of the belt through the buckle and sat with it in my lap. I had my weapon and even less time.

I'd have only one shot at this and I'd better make it a good one. If I missed, it was all over. I wouldn't have the strength to strangle him if he had an arm or leg in his teeth. I had to get him before he got me. What was it Arnie said, Attack the enemy's strength? There's a weakness there if you can only see it, and surprise itself is a weapon. I tried to see Hansi that way. An instinct-driven threshing machine. God, what I wouldn't give for his animal certainty. Everything is go or no go. Full tilt. I'm here stewing in my own juices. Scared shitless to do anything. All I could see was him clamping those jaws on me and tearing a huge chunk out of my throat, ripping it open like a wet grocery bag. Then a torrent of blood, spurting out until it just flowed and finally leaked out of me. What else could I do? Just wait for an icepick over the eye and a life not worth living? Why don't I just give him what he wants and get it over with? Just give him what he wants. I said that to myself again and a way out appeared in my mind.

This was my only chance. It had better work. I took a deep breath and let out some length on the looped belt I had in my lap. Now or never. I stood up. Hansi growled, bared his teeth and. . . . I fell to the floor with my throat bared.

I lay terribly still, barely able to control the twitches in my legs. Hansi stood still for a second and then slowly came over. I didn't move a muscle. I watched him out of the corner of my eye. He came closer. Then he was right next to me. I could feel the heat of his breath on my cheek. My hands were high on my chest, holding the noose I had for him. His ears were flattened, and his eyes were fixed on my throat. I knew he'd see my death in a black and white blur. I kept imagining it as an eternity of color. He pulled back his muzzle and I saw the row of interlocking teeth. Ivory blades set in black gums. A low growl came from his throat and the hot stink of his breath coated my face. I lay there with my throat bared while inches away Hansi stood stone still except for the incessant pulse of his heart and the quiver of his nostrils.

I slowly found myself breathing in the same rhythm as the dog. Very shallow and through my mouth. In and out. In and out. Waiting. Waiting. I had a weapon and an opportunity. If I could just find the will. I couldn't tear my eyes away from those awful teeth. The constant growl and the smell of death on his breath froze me. I was losing it. Hansi began to sit.

I jammed the noose over his head. Hansi pulled away, twisting his head to shake it off, but I had him. With both hands I pulled the noose tight. He twisted, whipping his head from side to side, pulling me across the floor on my belly and elbows. I pulled down on the noose, dragging his head to the floor. He twisted his neck from side to side, snapping at me with his teeth. I struggled up to my knees and yanked on the noose, throwing him over on his side. I leaned forward to wrap a loop around my fist. A paw flicked out and I pulled my face out of range. I was pulling the noose as tight as I could, but the dog didn't seem to be more than inconvenienced. The muscle sheath around his windpipe was enormous. He was still breathing easily, growling and ripping at the noose with his paws and teeth. He was in enough danger to be more concerned for himself than with coming after me. My hands were cramping. I didn't dare adjust my grip. The slightest release of pressure and he'd be on me in a flash. I staggered to my feet and pulled the dog across the room. I looked everywhere for something to use. My best bet was the high-backed desk chair. I dragged the dog over to it. He hadn't the brains to charge me and break the tension. He just kept pulling away and kept strangling himself. I hooked my leg around the chair and pushed it away from the desk. Dragging the belt over the top of the high-backed chair, I braced a foot against the seat and leaned back as if I was reeling in a fish. I pulled and the dog dug his claws into the carpet. Every muscle in my arms and back burned. I willed each one to tighten just one more notch. Slowly the dog came up off the floor. Thank god the chair was high enough. I wrapped another loop around my fist and leaned back. His hind legs were pedaling furiously in the air. The claws clicked frantically on the chair back. I held on. My arms were cramping and my hands were dead. I threw my head back and closed my eyes in furious prayer. Die, you son of a bitch. My whole body shook.

Finally I opened my eyes. The legs were still. The claws

silent. The dog swung slowly, stiffly. I unwrapped the belt from around my fists and lowered him to the floor. Trembling from exhaustion, I walked around and pulled the noose free from the dog's neck. It had been embedded deep enough to leave a permanent mark. The back of the chair was shredded where he had clawed at it, dying all the while.

I adjusted the loop to a man's size and walked over to the door. Thank god for soundproofing. I pulled open the door and stuck my head out. No one was in sight. I had to go back through the house to get out. I inched along the wall towards the staircase. Suddenly there was a shattering of glass, then the whump, whump of a silenced handgun. Maybe Samantha hadn't forgotten me. Glad it hadn't been an emergency though. I poked my head around the staircase and drew it back when I heard a burst of rapid-fire Spanish followed by feet pounding up the stairs. Then silence. This wasn't a coordinated ERT offensive. Whatever broke the glass wasn't tear gas. There were no bullhorn ultimatums. I really wanted to get out of this stairwell, which was no cover at all. I snaked around the stairs. What the hell was going on? Upstairs, there were rushing footsteps. Then silence. I had made it to the top of the staircase. I could see the front door only a few tantalizing strides away. There had been only one set of footsteps. Jesus probably going up to check out the noise. Where the hell were Ernesto and the others? Time to go before Jesus came back down. I took one last look around and Jesus came down the stairs pointing a silenced automatic at me. He motioned to me to come out of the stairwell. I stood up and walked towards him. My hands were held high. He moved gracefully down the stairs, his eyes scanning the foyer and the dining room off to my right. He motioned to me to step out into the center of the foyer. Jesus raised the gun from my chest to the middle of my face. I stared at the round black snout. His eyes were flatter than the dog's. There was no smile on his face, just a slight tilt of the head. That's life, he seemed to be saying. I thought about him blowing away James Tucker Calhoun, his mother and all the others, just as casually. I pursed my lips, and scoured the inside of my mouth with my tongue. I was going to put this gob of spit right in his eye even if it was, as I was sure it would be, the last thing I ever did.

Jesus thumbed back the hammer. I never opened my mouth. A whistling blur swept between us. I stared at Jesus. His eyes blinked rapidly then they began to flutter as he contemplated the blood spurting from the wrist where his gun hand had been. Jesus moaned weakly and clasped the stump to his chest. He looked at me, almost apologetically, as if he were saying, Look what I've done to myself. Could you help me? I was unmoved. He groaned and stroked his forearm, like it was a wounded animal and not a part of himself. The blood was only trickling out now and Jesus staggered back against the wall, slid to the floor and lay still.

Arnie stepped out of the shadows. I smiled weakly, unable to speak.

"Nice to see you too." His sword was still in his hand. He slowly drew the bloody blade through his palm, wiping it clean. He stared intently at it until he was satisfied by what he saw. He sheathed it again.

"I though I'd just bought the ranch. Whew." I exhaled and tried to get a deep breath, a cleansing breath. I felt polluted with fear. When I finally began to breathe easily, I looked up at Arnie and said, "Thanks." It was lame but words are of little use when we need them most. We shook hands slowly. That was enough.

"I guess Samantha called you, huh? I though that she'd gone off into spaceland and forgotten about the time. I was going to come back and haunt her. Erase all her disks."

"No. I just happened to call her right after you did. I'd found that guy for the Rev and I was right in the area. She gave me the address and I told her I'd call the cops if necessary. By the way, what did I interrupt here?"

"The persecution and death of Leo Haggerty as performed by the staff of the Snow Kings under the direction of Dr. Rolando Gutierrez, a.k.a. Colonel Bernardo Schmidt."

"Sounds very arty to me. How much were tickets?"

"Too much. In a nutshell, the guy who left me here with this guy—"

"And his buddy upstairs," Arnie interrupted.

"Has hypnotically programmed a boy to kill General Hortencio Villarosa tonight before he signs the treaty allowing us to send advisors to his country. The coke dealers who transport through his country with official approval have nixed the deal, so he has to go. I'm going to try to get down there and stop it. You want in?" I bent down and gingerly removed my Colt from Jesus's waistband and slipped it back into my shoulder rig.

Arnie looked at me and said, "What am I going to do here? Watch the meat cool?"

Chapter 32

I TOOK MY RECORDER and picks off Jesus's body and scooped up the files from the doctor's desk. Arnie had gone ahead to bring his car around. He arrived just as I reached the curb. When I opened the door to get in, he picked up a box from the passenger's seat and held it out to me.

"Want some pizza? It's mushroom and sausage. Your favorite."

I laughed. "No thanks, I'll pass. Maybe later."

Arnie pulled away and asked, "Where to?"

"InterAmerican Federation Building."

Fifteen minutes later we were parked opposite the I.A.F. building. The limousines were lined up in the circular driveway, dropping off men in medals and uniforms, and women in jewels and gowns. The security people were checking invitations, guest lists, picture I.D.s and so on. We had no chance of getting in that way.

"What now?" Arnie asked.

"We can't take this to the security people. The head of security is in on this. The building is international territory. Our police couldn't get in there if they wanted to." I pulled out my map of the place and stared at it. "Let's drive around, see what the back side looks like."

We drove past the well-lit formal gardens. You couldn't see much over the patterned concrete walls. On the second floor balcony, I saw men pacing back and forth. We drove to the end of the block. I kept staring at the map. Everything looked well-lit, locked up or patrolled.

"Why not try to buttonhole an American going in, tell

him what's going on, and see if he can warn Villarosa?"
Arnie asked.

"We may have to try that." I was busy matching up
details of the grounds with the map. Fences, walls, gates,
front fountain. Everything matched up. "Wait here. Let
me check something."

I jumped out and jogged over to the garden wall. The
service entrance gate was made of iron bars. There was
just one thing left to check out. I walked up to the gate
and looked up at the huge rear windows of the building.
The enormous crystal chandeliers backlit the men on the
balcony. My eyes scanned the layout of the gardens. It was
a maze of low hedges around a series of gazebos. Not an
unbroken straight line anywhere. I hurried back to the car.

"What'd you see?" Arnie asked.

"It's what I didn't see that's interesting. Put on the dome-
light."

I showed Arnie the map. "See this dotted black line
going from the main building through the garden?"

"Yeah?"

"Well, there's nothing in the garden that corresponds to
that dotted line."

"Okay. So?"

"So, look. The line continues from this building here to
the building over there."

Arnie looked up. "That's fine. But there's nothing there.
Just the street."

"Right. So what's there that you can't see?" I turned in
the seat to face him. Arnie sat there with his eyes flicking
from side to side, biting his lower lip. Then slowly he began
to smile. "A tunnel, perhaps?"

"What say we go find out?"

We drove around the corner and pulled up to one of the
side doors of the smaller building on the map. Casually,
we walked up to the door. I searched the glass panels for
imbedded alarm wires and found none. A sign above the
door said I.A.F. Adminstrative Annex. Arnie was looking
at the underside of the guttering for cameras. "No eyes,"
he said. Everything in the building was dark. There were

no guards to be seen. Thank god this was a public building and America had yet to fully terror-proof itself.

"Shall we?" Arnie said.

"After you, Alphonse."

He unwrapped a pick set like mine and selected a slim blade. A couple of turns left and right, a little pressure upwards and the door was open.

"Voila!"

After we slipped inside, I felt all over the frame for an alarm contact and found none. Once in the main corridor and away from the windows Arnie turned on a pencil flash. Halfway down the hall we saw a door marked Stairway, and we went through it. The door at the bottom was locked, but it too yielded to Arnie's gentle ministrations. Once through that we found ourselves in a corridor filled with boxes floor to ceiling. There was barely enough room to turn around. There must be a Parkinson's law of storage: Junk accumulates to fill the space available.

Arnie flashed the light around. To our left was a metal mesh gate with a sign, NO ADMITTANCE. There was also a large padlock to enforce the message. Arnie walked up to the gate, hooked his fingers through the mesh, and rattled the gate. He stepped back and said, "Piece of cake."

"Oh, Ollie. You've got a blowtorch up your sleeve?"

"Don't need it. Step back. We'll be through in a minute. Here, hold the light on the gate."

I took the flash and stepped back. Arnie walked up to the gate, turned around, and paced off several steps, all the while staring at the floor. I backed up with him. He looked up at the ceiling. "Okay." With that, he pulled his sword from its sheath. "Uh, Arnie, excuse me, that door is steel mesh and it's a good quarter-inch thick. You never told me that your blade was Excalibur."

"Ye of little faith."

Arnie held the sword, gripped in both hands, low over his right shoulder. He bounced on the balls of his feet, breathing deeply through his nose. Finally, with a shriek he dashed towards the door. Lunging forward, with his hands pulling down as if he were tossing a bag of grain, he snapped his wrists and the blade flashed through the links of the gate and buried itself in the floor. Slowly, tenderly, Arnie worked the blade free, ran his hand along its edge and apologized to it.

I pushed the gate open and followed the pencil flash into the darkness. There were exposed pipes running high along the left wall and little else. After I'd gone on a ways, I saw a vent in the ceiling. I stopped and shined the flash on it. Arnie felt the grate, then said, "I don't feel any air moving at all. It's totally closed at the other end. No use to us." We went on. We were probably under the gardens by now. On the right-hand wall we came to another steel mesh door. This one had a key lock. Behind it was a large electrical panel, sprouting wires in every direction. These were bundled into cables and disappeared into the wall around the panel.

"Looks interesting," Arnie said.

Arnie needed two tries to pick the lock. I flashed the light on the electrical panel.

"Looks like the main electrical panel for the building. If we cut the power here, it would give us the cover of darkness to work in," Arnie said.

"Great. Since I know what the boy and Gutierrez look like, I should be the one to go after them."

"Okay. Take the light with you and make sure the door to the main building's stairway is unlocked. Then bring it back to me. I'll need it when I flip these circuits and cut the cables."

"Right." I stopped then, trying to figure out how I'd get back to the door in the dark without killing myself.

"Count your steps," Arnie said grinning. "This is 218 from the door I cut through. I'll need to know how long to wait for you before I cut the lights."

I scurried down the tunnel as fast as I could. The door was locked but I was able to pick it. When I got back to Arnie I told him that it was seventy-nine steps to the door.

"Okay, remember the darkness will be a boon to this kid. If he's smart at all he'll move towards Villarosa in the dark, probably with this Gutierrez guy. Everyone else will probably be standing still. They've got no reason to try to go anywhere. See who's moving and try to get to the front of the line."

"Good point. What about you?"

"I'll retrace my steps and bring the car around to the front of the building. Once inside you're on your own."

"Yeah. I know."

"Leo, don't do anything stupid up there. You're just rearranging the dead, you know. If they don't whack Villarosa here it'll be somewhere else. And from what you said, the kid's in a rush to die. Don't go over the falls with him."

"Yeah, but he's been helped along quite a bit. I know what Gutierrez can do. The kid deserves a second chance. He's a tool and he doesn't even know it." I also knew the hold the dead can have over the living.

"Good luck then."

As I walked out of the range of Arnie's flash I counted up to seventy-nine in the darkness. I also reminded myself that if I did nothing, the treaty would fail and no American boys would die in Villarosa's country. All I had to do was trade in two deaths to prevent? forestall? thousands later. I stood in the darkness, my hand on the knob, imagining the different outcomes. Another wall, another stadium full of boys like Arnie had once been, or an aging dictator and a crew-cut kid who liked pizza and comic books, was afraid of girls and wanted to be a hero like his brother. I decided that if I was going to be haunted I preferred the dead to be nameless and faceless and that the chain between my deeds and their deaths be longer than the one whose links I could so easily count between myself and Marty Fernandez. When I turned the doorknob I heard a sputtering crackle and hiss behind me. Gun in hand I raced up the staircase in a darkness as complete as the one I had left behind.

A man's voice boomed out clearly, "Ladies and gentlemen, the general is very sorry for the inconvenience. We are looking into what the source of the trouble is right now and have called the electric company to try to restore power as soon as possible. In the meantime, for your safety, please be careful moving about and wait until we have been able to place candles in strategic places to provide some light."

Some couples were making use of the romantic potential of the situation. A number of men had taken out their lighters. In their glow I saw three or four men moving towards the exit doors. This stopped me for a second. Then I realized that if the security chief wanted to make the most of this cover, he'd send his men away from Villarosa and leave him isolated. I moved as quickly as I could without drawing attention to myself in the direction the other men had come from.

In the grand ballroom, I found the general standing alone by the punchbowl. Security had cleared out, giving Marty a clean shot. I was sure the general had been told that they were securing the perimeters. I pivoted to see if anyone else was in the room. A slim figure appeared in the doorway, then another. Gutierrez? Marty? I tightened my grip on my gun. If I saw the slightest movement I was going to shoot. I'd have to.

The lights went on. Villarosa, to my left, was dipping into the punchbowl. "It's about time," he said.

"That it is, general," Colonel Schmidt said.

Schmidt was standing at Marty's shoulder. Villarosa turned slowly, majestically and looked down at them along the ridge of that famous nose. Schmidt began to back away from Marty. Marty looked spaced-out and frightened.

I stepped up and said, "Hold it, Marty. Don't move." My gun was coming up when Schmidt threw his left arm around Marty's throat, reached into the boy's jacket, pulled out a revolver and held it to his head.

"Don't move, Haggerty, or dear Marty is a dead one."

I brought the muzzle up until it was aimed right at the center of Schmidt's face. "Do you think I care what happens to this asshole?" I wanted to keep Schmidt talking. You're less likely to pull the trigger when you're shooting off your mouth.

"Rolando, Rolando, what are you doing? I was gonna do it. I swear," Marty whimpered.

"Shut up, you fool," Schmidt sneered. "Drop your gun or I'll blow his head off."

"Not a chance, Schmidt. This time you're not walking away." Slowly, steadily, I closed the distance between us.

"That's far enough. I am walking out of here with the boy. Even if you shoot me, by reflex I'll pull the trigger and kill him, so back off."

"You've been watching too much T.V., colonel."

"Stop or I'll—" I shot Schmidt right in the face. His body flew backwards and slid spreadeagled across the floor, smearing a trail of blood and brains behind him. Marty collapsed in a heap. General Villarosa let out an enormous sigh.

An armed security man burst into the room. He looked at Schmidt and then at me. Our guns were trained on each other. Villarosa waved his hand at him and shouted, "Stop" before we shot each other.

"General," the security man said, "we must leave the building at once. It's an emergency. Another attempt on your life. Come now."

I bent down and scooped Marty up and slung him over my shoulder. The security man had holstered his pistol but kept his hand on its grip. As I hurried out alongside Villarosa, I saw a uniformed man scowling at us.

"General, who is that man?" I asked.

"Colonel Baranquilla, head of security. Why?"

"He's part of the plot to have you killed."

"I don't believe that."

"How come you were left standing alone when the lights went out? Baranquilla's idea, no?"

"Let's get out of here," Villarosa said.

We hurried across the foyer and down the front steps. All the guests were milling about on the lawn.

Villarosa's security people were herding the crowd away from the front doors. Beyond the gates, U.S. Capitol Police and D.C. police cars were lining up and officers were piling out. Villarosa stopped and spoke rapidly in Spanish to another uniformed officer. He and two other men disappeared. Later I learned that they had caught Baranquilla five feet this side of U.S. territory. Sometimes politics is a game of inches.

In the pushing and shoving, I meandered towards the invisible plane beyond which lay the beautiful U.S.A. Marty was still out. I crossed that invisible barrier between home and anywhere else and let out a deep sigh. A couple of D.C. cops approached me, hands on their guns.

"He's just passed out. There was a shooting inside and he was a hostage." I gently lowered Marty to the ground. "He hit his head pretty hard. You might want to get him a doctor. He might have a concussion."

I saw the general talking to a police officer and pointing at me. It was going to be a long night. Arnie came up alongside me. "Nice to see you made it out. This the kid?" He pointed at Marty.

"Yup, the one and only."

"What happened in there?"

"I got to Villarosa about the same time as Marty and Gutierrez, who is actually Schmidt, but that's a long story. Anyway I drew down on Marty and Gutierrez pulled a gun and used him as a shield when he tried to get away."

"And?"

"And he's lying inside drawing flies. Then a security guard came in and said that everyone had to leave the building. So we joined the crowd."

"That was my bright idea."

"What was?"

"When I came up out of the tunnel it finally occurred to me to practice what I preach—Go at their strength."

"Which is?"

"Making it hard to get in. So I made them want to come out." The Cheshire cat had nothing on him.

"Okay. How'd you do it?"

"What else? I phoned in a bomb threat."

Chapter 33

As I had promised Randi, Thanksgiving was celebrated at my house. She and Samantha were in the kitchen talking about writing while Arnie and I sipped our drinks on the porch. We hadn't talked since the shoot-out at the I.A.F. building.

"Didn't save much of anything did we?" I mused, not really expecting an answer.

General Hortencio Villarosa had signed the treaty the very next day and in less than a week American "advisors" were "in country." The first one died a week later, while on patrol. His name was Norman Powell and I saw his picture in the morning paper. There are no nameless, faceless dead.

"There was nothing you could do for the kid," Arnie said.

"Oh, I got him his second chance, that's for sure."

That second chance for Marty Fernandez was an admission to a psychiatric hospital where he was kept on a round-the-clock suicide watch. Four days later though, he leaped out of his new therapist's third floor office window and died instantly on the hood of a visitor's car forty feet below.

"You gave me a second chance too, remember?" Arnie reminded me.

"No. I wasn't smart enough for that. Samantha knew what you needed. A way to recoup your honor. That's why she told you where I was instead of calling the police." Arnie began to disagree but I waved him off. "No. She didn't tell me that. She wouldn't. I called the Rev. Your work for him was nowhere near Georgetown. In fact he told me that you'd delivered the guy to him at six A.M."

"It's what I am, Leo. The code is a part of me all the way through. I wish I could come all the way home, and sometimes it really hurts, like at the wall, but I have to accept that that's the price I pay, and for right now, I'm willing to pay it. Besides, I have friends who are willing to meet me halfway."

"That's right, you do, friend." Though I was smiling at his words, inside I remembered my lie to Samantha about what I was doing in Gutierrez's office. One day a lie like that would cost me more than it was worth. You can't have it all, Haggerty, I thought. When was I going to learn that?

Randi came out and told us that dinner was ready. I followed Arnie inside and took a moment to appreciate the bounty before us. Since Nate Grossbart had been able to extract the full death benefits due Marta Vasquez from her husband's life insurance policy, he gave me no more trouble than I expected when it came to paying my bill. A fair piece of that fee was on the table or in the oven or chilling in the refrigerator.

Samantha came up to me, kissed me on the cheek and whispered in my ear, "I've been in the kitchen talking to Randi."

"What about?"

"About writing, school, being a woman, boys and men— and you. You know how you said your work was as enduring as bubble gum? Think again. You'll be a part of that child forever. Like you're a part of me."

"I'm a lucky man indeed," I said and put my arm around her.

When we were all seated, I looked around at my makeshift family. They were not exactly what I had once envisioned but I was well blessed. Samantha suggested a moment of silence before we ate. We bowed our heads to give thanks. Through it all, though, I heard the sound of distant guns.